Cicero: De Imperio

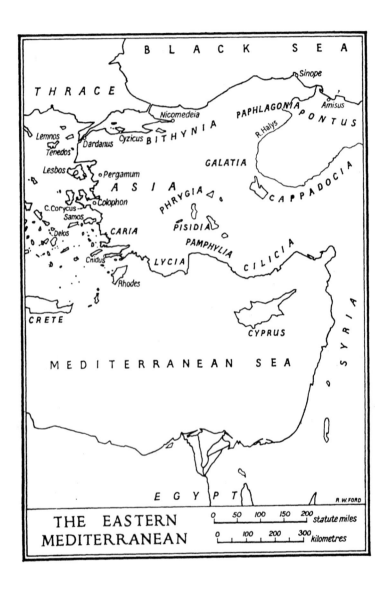

B L A C K   S E A

THRACE

Sinope

Nicomedeia

PAPHLAGONIA

Amisus

PONTUS

Lemnos

Cyzicus

BITHYNIA

R. Halys

Dardanus

Tenedos

Lesbos

GALATIA

Pergamum

ASIA

CAPPADOCIA

C. Corycus

Colophon

PHRYGIA

Samos

PISIDIA

Delos

CARIA

PAMPHYLIA

CILICIA

Cnidus

LYCIA

Rhodes

SYRIA

CRETE

CYPRUS

M E D I T E R R A N E A N   S E A

E G Y P T

R. W. FORD

THE   EASTERN
MEDITERRANEAN

0   50   100   150   200   statute miles

0   100   200   300   kilometres

CICERO

DE IMPERIO

Edited by

C. Macdonald

Bristol Classical Press

This impression 2005
This edition published in 1986 by
Bristol Classical Press
an imprint of
Gerald Duckworth & Co. Ltd.
90-93 Cowcross Street, London EC1M 6BF
Tel: 020 7490 7300
Fax: 020 7490 0080
inquiries@duckworth-publishers.co.uk
www.ducknet.co.uk

A catalogue record for this book is available
from the British Library

ISBN 0 86292 182 1

Cover illustration: Cicero from a portrait bust,
Vatican Museum, Rome.

CONTENTS

v

PREFACE

THIS is a speech which has appeal both for the pupil tackling a work of Cicero for the first time and for the more advanced student. In style it is one of the best of its type and its subject-matter is almost always interesting without being obscure. Furthermore, it introduces the reader to a variety of historical events and political activity at Rome such as would be difficult to find in any other single work of moderate length.

This edition aims at providing the essential background information for an intelligent reading of the text, but does not seek to do all the pupil's reading for him. It is hoped that some of the notes, necessarily allusive in an edition of this length, will encourage him to further study on his own.

The notes try to do three things. Firstly, they hope to show the reader how to tackle passages rather more difficult than the majority of the speech without relieving him of all responsibility, but where convenient opportunities offer they provide a finished translation to guide the reader for the future. Secondly, notes upon matters of syntax and accidence — some quite elementary — are provided, not to give a label to passages likely to prove attractive to examiners, but to assist in accurate translation and to try to explain the construction. Thirdly, there is provided a considerable amount of information upon the historical and political background. These notes contain much of the most interesting material in the book, but here, too, every

GERM

GALLIA

CISALPINE GAUL
Vercellae○
TRANSALPINE GAUL
○Aquae Sextiae

Illyria

ITA

Picenum

R. Tiber
Rome
Ostia
Caieta
Capua
APPHA

CORSICA

Tyrrhenian Sea

○Numantia

NEARER ○Saguntum

M·D

SARDINIA

FURTHER
SPAIN

SPAIN

M   E   D   I   T   E   R

Drepana
SICILY
Syracuse
C.Pachynus

Messana

MAURETANIA

NUMIDIA

A

Vetus provincia

Carthage

A   F   R   I   C

GAETULI

0   100   200   300   400   500 statute miles
0   200   400   600 kilometres

THE ROMAN WORLD

effort has been made to incite to further reading rather than to let the length of notes become excessive. It will be found that, in general, assistance is given rather more fully at the beginning of the speech.

The reader is not burdened with references to the work of modern scholars in the text. There is instead a bibliographical note which gives guidance concerning the books which can conveniently be consulted for further information. This note, however, is by no means exhaustive and I am deeply conscious of the debt I owe to many whose names do not appear in that note. The debt is obvious throughout this edition and I gladly take this opportunity of acknowledging it.

C. M.

INTRODUCTION

I. LIFE OF CICERO

MARCUS TULLIUS CICERO was born at Arpinum, a Volscian hill-town, on 3rd January 106 B.C. and was killed on 7th December 43 on the instructions of M. Antonius. His family was well-to-do and had links with senatorial circles in Rome. His father, a member of the Equestrian Order, was a man of literary tastes and took Marcus and Quintus, his younger brother, to Rome where they were given a good schooling. Marcus proved an apt pupil and continued to show interest in literary and philosophical studies throughout his life. In 91 he assumed the *toga virilis* and two years later saw military service for a short time under Cn. Pompeius Strabo in the Social War fought against the rebellious Italian allies. It is reasonable to assume that in the course of this service he met Strabo's son, the young Pompey, who was serving with his father in this fighting. In the following year he was living at Rome studying philosophy and rhetoric under the leading teachers of the day and in his studies would have got to know the other young men who were destined later to become leading figures in Roman political life. He attached himself to Quintus Mucius Scaevola the Augur and, on his death, to Scaevola the Pontifex Maximus. He heard the famous orators of the day, M. Antonius and L. Crassus, and attended the lectures of Apollonius Molon, the rhetorician.

His first speech was *pro Quinctio* in 81 and there followed in 80 his plea *pro Sexto Roscio Amerino*. In the following year he left Rome for the East and was absent for two years. He spent some time in Athens, visited Asia Minor and the island of Rhodes, where he had further instruction from Molon and from the philosopher Posidonius.

Returning to Rome in 77 he appeared in a number of important cases and it was at this time that he married his wife Terentia, who, probably in the following year, bore him his daughter Tullia. It was in this year too that his official career began with his election to the quaestorship. The next year saw him at Lilybaeum in Sicily where he proved himself an upright and honest official under a good governor who was, unfortunately for the Sicilians, succeeded by the infamous Verres. Cicero's ability and industry in securing Verres's conviction for extortion led to the *lex Aurelia* of 70, which deprived the senators of two-thirds of the membership of the juries which they had held since the Sullan legislation. His success in this case also established his reputation as the equal of his senior colleague, Hortensius. The office of curule aedile followed in 69 and three years later he became praetor and in this speech, his first *contio*, supported the Manilian law. Throughout this period he was speaking in cases at Rome, as was essential for a man with political ambitions, and he hoped in return for this speech to be nominated for the consulship by Pompey. In the event he was to wait a further three years before becoming consul and was only elected for 63 because his chief opponent, L. Sergius Catilina, was regarded by the senators as a dangerous revolutionary and Cicero as a safe moderate.

In the consular elections for 62 Catiline was again an unsuccessful candidate and Cicero's disclosure to the Senate of the impending rebellion in Etruria forced Catiline to leave Rome. The other conspirators who remained in the city were betrayed by the envoys of the Allobroges, a Gallic tribe from whom they had sought support, arrested, and, after a debate in the Senate upon their fate, were executed. In the new year Catiline and his army were brought to battle and annihilated.

Cicero devoted the end of this decade to his attempts at reconciling the divergent interests of *equites* and Senate in a *concordia ordinum*, but any success he had was short-lived. Pompey returned from his victories in the East only to find his political ambitions thwarted by the Senate in spite of the support he received from Cicero. Turning from the Senate he therefore formed his secret alliance with Crassus and Julius Caesar, the consul-elect for 59. This coalition became known as the First Triumvirate and at the end of the year Cicero was invited to become a fourth member. After long delay he finally refused the offer and in 59 retired from public life, thus rejecting the appointments which would have brought him security and would have prevented his banishment in 58 by the law of the tribune Clodius. To agree meant linking himself with a man who was in his eyes a potential revolutionary, and submitting to the Triumvirs' will. This Cicero was not prepared to do, and he preferred to go into an exile from which he was recalled by law in 57 and granted compensation.

There was no positive policy common to the three members of the Triumvirate, with the result that their alliance of mutual convenience tended to fall apart as soon as the pressures which had welded them together were relaxed. Cicero spent the months following his return in private practice at the Bar, but a move on his part and by political colleagues against Caesar's interests brought a swift reaction from the threatened partner. The Triumvirate was patched up at the Conference of Luca in 56 and Cicero was given the choice of doing the Triumvirs' will or taking the consequences of his disobedience. This ultimatum resulted in his speech *de provinciis consularibus* with its lavish praise of Caesar and for the remainder of the decade until the outbreak of the Civil War Cicero remained on reasonably friendly terms with both Caesar and Pompey. This dual allegiance, however, became increasingly difficult. The death of Crassus in the Battle of Carrhae in 53 and the death of Caesar's daughter Julia, who was married to Pompey, removed two of the links holding Caesar and Pompey together and as they drew apart Cicero inclined more and more to Pompey.

During the years between 52 and 46 Cicero made few speeches in either courts or Senate, and in 51 was the unwilling proconsul of Cilicia, an office forced upon him by a temporary shortage of eligible ex-magistrates caused by Pompey's legislation aimed at discouraging extortion in the provinces. From his year's absence he hurried back to a city faced with inevitable civil war. After hesitation he joined the Pompeian forces, but when the fighting was over made his peace with the victorious Caesar. Though severely disapproving of

Caesar's unconstitutional rule, he had no part in the dictator's murder.

In February 45 he had suffered the bitter blow of his beloved Tullia's death and consoled himself with an intense literary activity in which he was immersed when Caesar died. He now became bitterly opposed to Caesar's successor, Antony, and in the autumn of 44 delivered the first of his violent attacks upon him which, in imitation of Demosthenes's attacks upon Philip of Macedon, he called *Philippics*. The last of this series was delivered in April 43, and of the remaining months of his life we know little. Livy tells us that he faced death bravely and his estimate of the man, preserved for us by Seneca, is as just as any: ' si quis tamen virtutibus vitia pensaret, vir magnus et memorabilis fuit, et in cuius laudes exsequendas Cicerone laudatore opus fuerit.'

2. ROMAN ORATORY

The Romans were, as in almost every sphere of intellectual activity, deeply indebted to the Greeks for their development of oratory as a literary genre. The idea of oratory as an art was well established in Rome by the beginning of the first century and the Roman pupils of the Greek rhetoricians followed their masters in adopting the threefold classification of *eloquentia* into the simple, ornate, and middle styles (*tenuis* or *exilis*, *grandis* or *ornata*, and *media*).

The simple or Attic style was descended from Lysias, who composed his speeches in a form which paid particular attention to brevity, directness, and clarity.

All verbal extravagance and any over-elaborate phraseology were carefully avoided. There were some orators, known as the *novi Attici*, following these precepts during this period, and the leading exponents of this group were C. Licinius Calvus and M. Brutus. Their speeches, however, do not seem to have aroused the enthusiasm of their audiences and did not long hold their place in men's memories. This style, indeed, must have lacked warmth and inspiration. Latin would prove a less apt medium for its exponents than Attic Greek, and without a certain amount of ornament and departure from the norms of everyday life it is a dull and graceless language.

In contrast with this extreme simplicity there also at this time flourished an Asiatic school. Hortensius was its leader, but no example of his work, nor of that of any Asianist, survives. We can, however, learn much about it from Cicero's criticisms. He distinguishes two styles, one *sententiosum et argutum* and the other *verbis volucre atque incitatum*. Its chief characteristics were an emphasis on antithesis and as many ingenious turns of thought or phrase, called by the Romans *sententiae*, as possible. The language was high-flown and the vocabulary that of poetry rather than of everyday speech. There was also a straining after rhythmical effects. It is easy to understand how readily so extravagant a style could degenerate into utter artificiality and a mere cleverness often quite inappropriate to the matter in hand.

Cicero steered a middle course between the two extremes. He took as his model Demosthenes, but his was no slavish imitation. He well knew how far apart in character stood Athenian and Roman and how different were the Greek and Latin languages. He insisted upon the accurate use of vocabulary and idiom, carefully avoiding all that was unusual. His style was plain and unadorned when this was appropriate, but in his view it was essential for a good orator at times to attempt something more, and then ornament was certainly required.

His greatest achievements were the development of the 'period', and the adoption and extension of one of the Asiatic school's most important adornments, the use of a clearly defined rhythm before a break in the sense. The Polish scholar Zielinski has analysed these endings and found the commonest to be a cretic and trochee or spondee ($-\cup--\stackrel{\scriptscriptstyle\cup}{}$). Other final rhythms are a cretic or molossus followed by a trochee and doubtful syllable ($-\stackrel{\scriptscriptstyle\cup}{}--\cup\stackrel{\scriptscriptstyle\cup}{}$), a cretic and a double trochee ($-\stackrel{\scriptscriptstyle\cup}{}--\cup-\cup$). Long syllables can be resolved (e.g. $-\cup\stackrel{\scriptscriptstyle\cup\cup}{}-\cup$ gives the famous *esse videatur*) and sometimes the cretic is followed by spondees to give a solemn effect ($-\stackrel{\scriptscriptstyle\cup}{}-----$).

This speech contains a variety of rhetorical figures. The notes show how their use affects Cicero's meaning but, for convenience, some examples are listed below:

1. **Antithesis.** The contrast of opposites.
    2. Ita . . . consecutus.
    12. Videte ne, **ut** . . . , **sic** . . .
2. **Chiasmus.** The a:b, b:a order of contrasting words.
    10. **felicitati** . . . **virtuti** . . . , **culpae**, . . . **fortunae.** . . .
3. **Commutatio.** The reversal of two words or phrases to give a different meaning.
    31. . . . quis umquam arbitraretur aut **ab omnibus**

imperatoribus uno anno aut **omnibus annis** ab **uno imperatore** confici posse?

    67. Ecquam putatis civitatem **pacatam** fuisse, quae **locuples** sit? ecquam esse **locupletem**, quae istis **pacata** esse videatur?

    4. Enallage. The use of one number for another.

    9. . . . ac litteras misit ad eos **duces**, . . .

    33. ex Miseno autem eius ipsius **liberos**, . . .

    5. Metonomy. The use of a related word to convey the meaning of another.

    32. . . . , cum duodecim **secures** in praedonum potestatem pervenerint?

    6. Parataxis. The co-ordinate arrangement of two clauses of which the first is only required for the sake of obtaining a contrast.

    58. An . . . potuerunt: . . .

    63. . . . , illorum auctoritatem . . . praeponeretis.

    7. Praeteritio. The device in which the speaker states that he will omit certain material which he then immediately goes on to mention.

    48. Itaque **non sum praedicaturus,** . . .

    60. **Non dicam** hoc loco, . . .

    8. Traductio. The repetition of a word in close juxtaposition with different meanings attached to it.

    1. . . . , omne meum **tempus** amicorum **temporibus** transmittendum putavi.

    62. Quae in omnibus **hominibus** nova post **hominum** memoriam constituta sunt, ea tam multa non sunt quae haec, quae in hoc uno **homine** vidimus.

3. DE IMPERIO CN. POMPEI AD QUIRITES ORATIO

Outline of the Speech

Exordium. The introduction: 1–3.

Narratio. The statement of the situation: 4–5.

Confirmatio. The speaker makes his case: 6–50.

The nature of the war: 6–19.

The size of the war: 20–26.

How to choose a general: 27–50.

Confutatio. Refutation of opponents: 51–67.
Conclusio. The summing-up: 69–71.

Cicero himself regarded this speech as a masterpiece of the *medium dicendi genus*. He says (*Orator*, 101): ' is erit igitur eloquens, qui poterit parva summisse, modica temperate, magna graviter dicere. Fuit ornandus in Manilia lege Pompeius; temperata oratione ornandi copiam persecuti sumus.' The speech is also of particular interest to us for the clarity with which its subject-matter is arranged.

The original title of the speech is in some doubt. It is known either as *de imperio Cn. Pompei*, which would appear to conflict with the Latin of the passage quoted in the previous paragraph, or as *pro lege Manilia*, but the regular usage of *pro* is to mean ' on behalf of ' a client, not a measure. It has been suggested that the title may originally have been *de lege Manilia*.

4. ROME AND THE EAST

The Second Century. Rome emerged from the Second Punic War as the mistress of the western Mediterranean. In the East lay the successor kingdoms of the empire of Alexander the Great and even though the Senate at Rome had no wish to see any expansion of Rome's overseas territories, yet her increased status as a Mediterranean power made contact inevitable. It was not long before Rome was drawn into the affairs of the Greek world. At the beginning of the second century the cities of Greece were attacked by Antiochus of Syria and Philip of Macedon, and they turned to

Rome for help. Rome intervened against Philip, who had sided with the Carthaginians in the Second Punic War, and defeated him in the Second Macedonian War (200–196). She then withdrew but soon had to return to Greece to deal with an invasion by Antiochus. He, in his turn, was ejected and Rome once again left the Greeks to run their own affairs, even after Philip's son Perseus had involved her in a Third Macedonian War (171–167). But she now found that permanent withdrawal from an arena in which she was steadily becoming the leading power was impossible, and that the only way to stop the Greeks from fighting among themselves and to bring stability to the kingdom of Macedonia was to step in and impose her own direct government upon the area. She therefore formed the new province of Macedonia in 146.

Thirteen years later Rome's empire in the East received another substantial addition. King Attalus III of Pergamum died leaving no heir to inherit his kingdom, which was at that time in a disturbed state. Before his death he had made a will in which he named the Roman people as his heirs in the hope that future trouble would be prevented. When he died in 133 Rome accepted the legacy and ratified the will, but before a senatorial commission under Scipio Nasica could carry out their organization of the new province, a revolt broke out under the leadership of Aristonicus, an illegitimate son of Attalus's predecessor, Eumenes. Rome appealed for help to the neighbouring kings but only in 131 did Licinius Crassus lead a Roman force against him. Crassus was killed before he could do much, but the consul of the following year, M. Perperna, defeated and captured Aristonicus. It was, however, left to Manius Aquilius, consul in 129, to complete the work of the senatorial commission. The largest part of the kingdom was annexed and formed into the new Roman province of Asia. Some of the poorer eastern districts were handed back to the local rulers, while in the province itself, some of the Greek cities, including Pergamum, were left free but others had to pay tribute.

The Rise of Pontus. The dynasty of Mithridates had ruled in Pontus from the end of the fourth century, but after two centuries of their rule the country still remained one of villages rather than of cities, even though the Greek inhabitants had done much to hellenize the native aristocracy. The kings, however, were as proud of their descent from the Persian royal family as they were of their Greek training. The two elements were never fully combined and each played its part in the policy of the Pontic kings.

In 151 Mithridates V Euergetes came to the throne and followed a policy of friendship towards Rome while at the same time he enlarged his kingdom. He helped Rome against Carthage and against the Pergamene pretender, Aristonicus, and received Phrygia as his reward. He had already acquired Galatia, inherited Inner Paphlagonia, and, by putting his son-in-law on the throne, gained control of Cappadocia. After a reign of thirty years he was assassinated, and his alleged will named his wife and two small sons as his successors. One of these was Mithridates Eupator, who removed his mother and brother from the scene to become the sole ruler of a kingdom considerably smaller than it had been before his father's death. The Romans, suspicious of its growing strength, had reduced it to the size that it had been before the time of Aristonicus and the acquisition of Cappadocia and Paphlagonia.

Mithridates made the first extension to his empire along the north coast of the Black Sea. The Greek cities established along that coast had appealed to Mithridates for protection against the Scythians and Sarmatians. Mithridates answered their calls for help and sent a series of expeditions to their aid, with the result that these cities were absorbed into the Pontic kingdom.

At the same time Mithridates extended his rule along the southern shore. He occupied Lesser Armenia and converted it into a stronghold for the rest of the kingdom. The city of Trapezus and kingdom of Colchis followed Armenia and his control over the Black Sea was now complete.

He next turned his attention to Asia Minor and, having come to an arrangement with Nicomedes, king of Bithynia, he began to carve an empire for himself out of the lands of his neighbours. The two kings absorbed Paphlagonia, occupied Galatia, and then moved against Cappadocia, but at this juncture the conquerors parted company and Nicomedes played his ally false by suddenly occupying the country. Mithridates, however, did not long tolerate this treachery and quickly ejected his former ally. He then consolidated his hold over the country by murdering Ariarthes the king and placing his own son upon the throne. Nicomedes, by now fearful for his own safety, appealed to Rome and gained a sympathetic hearing since the Senate felt that the time had come to stop this expansion of power; the two kings were told to leave

Paphlagonia and Cappadocia alone. Mithridates now
tried a new means of expanding his power. He married
his daughter to Tigranes, king of Armenia, who in 93
invaded Cappadocia and installed a figurehead of
Mithridates upon the throne. Rome again intervened,
and Sulla, now propraetor of Cilicia, restored Ariobarzanes, the rightful ruler. Thus Mithridates was again
thwarted and it must by now have become clear to him
that a clash with Rome was inevitable so long as the
Senate was prepared to dictate its will in Asia Minor.
The First Mithridatic War. The time was now ripe
for Mithridates to move again, for two reasons. Firstly,
Rome was deeply committed in the war with her
Italian allies and, secondly, the death of Nicomedes
and the quarrels amongst his sons which followed had
removed his only serious rival to power in Asia Minor.
Mithridates, therefore, placed his candidate upon the
throne of Bithynia and in conjunction with Tigranes
again drove Ariobarzanes from Cappadocia. The
dispossessed kings appealed to Rome and Mithridates
was told to restore Nicomedes IV to Bithynia, and the
two fugitives were reinstated. Indeed Nicomedes,
urged on by Roman greed, passed to the offensive and
raided the Paphlagonian coast. Mithridates's protest
was ignored and he was told to evacuate Cappadocia
and leave Nicomedes alone.
　　These instructions were followed by a Roman invasion of Mithridates's empire mounted with the
assistance of Nicomedes. The Roman forces met with
disaster on all fronts, and Mithridates after entering
Bithynia overran the Roman province. At first considerable resistance was offered to him by a number of

the Greek cities, but once the possibility of Roman protection had vanished they greeted Mithridates as the liberator of Asia. As an instrument of deliberate policy in order to convince the province still more deeply that Roman rule was at an end, Mithridates ordered the simultaneous massacre of all Romans and Italians to the number of 80,000. He then proceeded to an unsuccessful assault on Rhodes which was providing a refuge for those Romans who had escaped from the province, but even before this attack he had carried the war into Greece. Athens was occupied, and it looked as if the whole of Greece would fall into his hands. The Romans, however, succeeded in checking his advance at Chaeronea where Mithridates's general, Archelaus, was compelled to retreat into Attica. The arrival of the quaestor L. Lucullus with the first troops of Sulla's army eased matters, but Sulla's position after his arrival was dangerous for some time. He moved first to the elimination of the enemy's strongholds in Attica and on 1st March 86, after a bitter siege, Athens fell. He then turned to the Peiraeus and when it was captured he was free to march north. He met the Pontic forces under Archelaus in two battles—at Chaeronea and Orchomenus—and won a resounding victory on both occasions. The invasion of Greece was over and these victories produced a rapid change of heart in the cities of Asia. Many revolted from Mithridates's rule, as did Galatia, and negotiations for peace were opened between Sulla and Archelaus.

In the first half of 85 the position of Mithridates grew rapidly worse. Fimbria was fighting a most successful campaign and, advancing from Bithynia, he drove the king in flight before him. This chance of capturing the king was lost owing to the intrusion of Roman politics: Lucullus, a follower of Sulla, refused to co-operate with Fimbria who had been a strong supporter of Marius. Lucullus had been sent out to the East in the winter of 87–86 to raise a fleet, and had been fomenting revolts among the islands and along the coast of Asia Minor. In August 85 Mithridates accepted Sulla's terms in the Peace of Dardanus, was reconciled to Nicomedes and Ariobarzanes, and returned to Pontus.

Sulla now devoted his energies to the settlement of the affairs of Asia Minor. Fimbria's army was deserting in considerable numbers to Sulla's forces and was disbanded, loyal states were rewarded, Nicomedes and Ariobarzanes restored to their thrones, hostile cities reduced, and the followers of the king punished. For the coming winter Sulla billeted his troops upon the province and fixed an indemnity of 20,000 talents. In 84 he left Murena with two of Fimbria's legions to control the province, and himself, after a short stay of a few months in Greece, sailed with his army for Italy.

The Second Mithridatic War. Mithridates spent the months following the end of the war in reorganizing his kingdom and suppressing revolts in the north. Murena viewed with displeasure the large force raised for one of these expeditions against the inhabitants of the Cimmerian Bosporus, because the whole of the kingdom of Cappadocia had not yet been returned to Ariobarzanes. Murena feared, or so he made out, that these preparations were for war against Rome, and Archelaus appeared at his headquarters to increase his suspicions. On this pretext, at any rate, he marched through

Cappadocia and attacked Comana. The king appealed to the Treaty of Dardanus but Murena maintained that since it was not yet in writing it did not exist. He then made a further raid across the Halys and advanced on Sinope. Mithridates gathered his forces, and his generals forced the withdrawal of Murena who was then decisively defeated by the king in person and the Romans retreated rapidly into Phrygia. All the Roman garrisons were driven from Cappadocia and Mithridates was about to follow up his successes when an order came from Sulla to Murena to refrain from further hostilities, and to Mithridates to be reconciled to Ariobarzanes. Both orders were obeyed and Ariobarzanes lost part of Cappadocia to Mithridates, while Murena was hailed as *imperator* and celebrated what must be one of the least-deserved triumphs in Roman history.

The Third Mithridatic War. Mithridates, freed from Murena's raids, now returned to the task of recovering his Bosporan possessions. After a disastrous expedition he returned to his kingdom where he was ordered by Sulla to return the rest of Cappadocia. The king obeyed and sent an embassy to Rome to ratify the Peace of Dardanus, but before it arrived Sulla had died and it could obtain no satisfaction from the Senate. Mithridates therefore incited his son-in-law, Tigranes, to occupy Cappadocia.

In a struggle with Rome Mithridates could rely for help on the Cilicians as well as on Tigranes, and he could expect that the Egyptians and Cyprus would be benevolent neutrals. Further afield, his agents in Europe were causing trouble among the tribes along the border of Macedonia, and at the other end of the

Mediterranean he sought an alliance with Sertorius in Spain.

To both sides war seemed inevitable. Rome kept four legions in Asia Minor and once again the *casus belli* was to be provided by the Bithynian succession. Nicomedes IV died leaving no heir and Rome declared Bithynia a province, but it was intolerable to Mithridates that the entrance to the Black Sea should pass into Roman hands. He therefore declared himself the protector of a claimant to the throne and marched through Paphlagonia to invade Bithynia and at the same time sent a force into Cappadocia.

The Romans were caught at a disadvantage owing to the recent death or incompetence of their provincial governors, and only after much intrigue were the consuls of 74 appointed, M. Aurelius Cotta to Bithynia and L. Lucullus to the command of the forces in Asia and Cilicia. The appointment of Lucullus was sensible, since he knew Asia Minor well and was the most capable commander available in the absence of Pompey. It was not long, however, before Cotta was defeated, and Mithridates advanced rapidly to invade the province of Asia from the north. He besieged Cyzicus, which he regarded as the gateway to the province, but Lucullus compelled him to raise the siege and his retreating army was annihilated. Thus ended the first stage of the campaign with the loss by Mithridates of the whole of his initial conquests and a large part of both his army and his fleet.

Having eventually reached Amisus safely, Mithridates requested help from Tigranes, the Bosporans, and even from the Scythians and Parthians. His potential allies proved lukewarm but the king addressed himself to the task of defending his kingdom with vigour. Cotta, Lucullus, and his lieutenant, C. Valerius Triarius, joined forces at Nicomedeia and prepared for the invasion of Pontus.

Lucullus began his advance into Pontus in the summer of 73 and, crossing the Halys, marched on Amisus. His advance was hindered by the enemy cavalry, and a number of engagements was fought, in the last of which Mithridates was nearly killed and his army cut to pieces. The king only saved himself from capture by the Roman cavalry with the ruse of scattering some treasure in their line of advance. He abandoned his kingdom and took refuge with Tigranes. Cabeira now surrendered to Lucullus and he spent there the winter of 72–71. Armenia Minor was reduced, Amisus and Sinope captured, and the conquest of Pontus completed by 70.

Before returning to the attack Lucullus spent his time in Asia reorganizing the province. He curtailed the extortions of the money-lenders and put the province on a sound financial footing, thereby earning the enduring hatred of the financiers at Rome, who left no stone unturned in their efforts to remove him from his command.

A request to Tigranes to surrender Mithridates was ignored, and in 69 Lucullus therefore marched upon Armenia. He received supplies from Ariobarzanes and marched through Cappadocia to the Euphrates and then on to the Tigris. Tigranes was taken by surprise, and a force sent out to deal with Lucullus was destroyed. In the ensuing confusion Lucullus made for Tigranocerta

and laid siege to it. Tigranes completed his mobiliza-
tion and advanced against Lucullus who marched out
to meet him. The Armenians were utterly defeated and
Tigranocerta captured. Much of Tigranes's kingdom
now came over to the Romans and Tigranes made an
offer to restore all the territory recently captured.

The troops of Lucullus at this juncture refused to
march any further and the shortcomings of Lucullus
as a leader of men began to affect his campaign. His
position, moreover, was made even more difficult by
his equestrian enemies in Rome who said that he was
prolonging the war for his own ends, and eventually
the government withdrew him from the province of
Asia. Q. Marcius Rex, the consul of 68, was appointed
to succeed him the following year in Cilicia, but even
though his troops were war-weary, Lucullus made
preparations for a further attack upon Tigranes.

Tigranes was joined by Mithridates, and late in the
summer of 68 Lucullus set out for the north to march
on Artaxata, the capital of Armenia proper, in order to
force Tigranes to fight. During the march Mithridates
appeared on the scene, ready to offer battle, and
Lucullus in the engagement which followed put his
army to flight. The climatic rigours, however, proved
too much for his men and in the end they refused to
move. His discipline had been weakened by the attacks
made upon him 'at Rome and by the current rumours
that he had been replaced. As soon as Lucullus retired
from the Armenian uplands Tigranes and Mithridates
struck. Mithridates advanced into Pontus but Lucullus,
now reinforced by Triarius, forced him to withdraw,
and both armies went into winter quarters.

xxx INTRODUCTION

Mithridates was on the move again early in 67 and, luring Triarius into attacking him, inflicted a defeat upon him. Lucullus arrived on the scene soon after and tried to bring Mithridates to battle, but he was unsuccessful and Mithridates retired to await Tigranes. The troops from Fimbria's army were now in open mutiny, and Lucullus appealed for help to Marcius Rex, the proconsul of Cilicia, but he refused on the grounds that his troops would not march. M'. Acilius Glabrio refused to move beyond the boundaries of Bithynia, and Lucullus was thus compelled to remain inactive while Mithridates recovered most of his kingdom and Tigranes plundered Cappadocia.

The Romans were right to appoint Pompey to finish his task, but it is fair to say that Lucullus was the real conqueror of Mithridates. He was a great tactician and imaginative strategist, but not a great leader of men. His discipline was too consistently exacting and he demanded too much of them without having sufficient thought for their well-being. Under his command the war would never have been fought to a finish.

5. THE POLITICAL BACKGROUND

To understand many of the references to contemporary politics in this speech and why it was a tribunician bill that Cicero was supporting, we must look at the development of the Roman constitution since the end of the third century and know something of the constitutional struggles that had been in progress for the past sixty or seventy years.

There had emerged from the early struggle of the

orders between patrician and plebeian a tripartite constitution, of which the constituent parts were: the executive represented by the magistrates, the administrative Senate, and the popular assemblies who held the electoral and legislative power. These three elements were theoretically equal, but the Senate in fact played a dominant role. This, as we shall see, became even more marked at the end of the third and beginning of the second centuries as Rome grew from an Italian city-state to a Mediterranean power.

At first sight the magistrates and assemblies may seem to have a claim for parity with the Senate. The consuls summoned and presided over the Senate, and a president can do much to guide a body towards the decision he desires. In time of war, too, the consuls had a very wide range of power, but they were themselves life-members of the Senate and most were reluctant to oppose the policies of the majority. Similarly, it might appear that, since in the popular assemblies the people were sovereign and since they indirectly controlled the composition of the Senate through the magisterial elections, they were in practice as well as theory constitutionally the Senate's equal. But this was not so. The Roman people were electorally conservative and resolutely continued to elect to the magistracies the members of a few noble families. Nor do they seem to have asserted their right to control fiscal measures or other financial legislation. The Senate's control in this sphere was of long standing and was not questioned until the time of the Gracchi.

The acquiescence by the people in senatorial domination was carried a stage further in the wars of the last decades of the third century. It resulted from the senatorial stout-heartedness and the inability of a scattered and ill-informed people to have any effective control over the administration of home affairs or foreign ties. The Senate's authority in both these fields gave it a position of extraordinary importance for a body which should only have been giving advice to magistrates.

This increase in the Senate's authority gathered momentum. *Senatus consulta* began to have force without ratification, and the control of foreign affairs enabled the Senate to manoeuvre the people into positions in which withdrawal from proposed hostilities was impossible. Thus was removed from the people for all practical purposes the right to declare war, and this infringement of their rights was naturally followed by their losing control of the conduct of wars and of the imposition of peace terms.

The strength of the senatorial position in the conduct of foreign affairs was notably improved by the decision of Rome in 200 to enter, in consort with several other powers, the war against Philip V of Macedon. The Senate, used to dealing with the contingents of Italian *socii*, showed little hesitation in directing the federation of allies, a direction that became more brusque as Roman power increased. This increasing control over other states brought great prestige at home and abroad and it was with the Senate, not the assemblies, that kings, cities and peoples dealt, and the terms on which they dealt were the Senate's.

There were three ways, however, in which the senatorial control could be challenged. Firstly, there was always the danger of powerful individuals rising up from among the Senate's own ranks. Secondly, its position rested upon popular acquiescence and although the conservative Roman temperament and political astuteness of the Senate made it more difficult for the people to reassert their rights the longer their acquiescence lasted, yet those rights were still generally acknowledged. Thirdly, and most important, there was that relic of the days of the patrician monopoly of political power, the tribunate.

It seems that about the middle of the second century all three dangers started to press upon the Senate. The first source of opposition, that from within their own ranks, the senators were able to deal with by legislation. The requirement of a period of ten years between consular terms of office, and the *lex Villia annalis* which saw that men did not come to high office too young, together with a later law prohibiting second consulships, went far to curbing the ambitions of able and energetic senators. The long Spanish wars from 154 to 133, with their constant drain upon the free Italian manpower, brought in their train popular discontent with the Senate's conduct of affairs. We find that this discontent led to the people forcing the Senate to disregard the *lex Villia annalis* and the ten year gap between consulships. There is clear evidence of violent anti-senatorial feeling in the 140's and 130's, and this feeling was led by the tribunes.

The tribunate had justified its continued existence after its original purpose had disappeared by allowing itself to be turned by the Senate into an invaluable brake upon the combination of magistrate and people which the Senate had no effective power to thwart, however strong its feelings against a bill might be. The use of the tribunician veto in the Senate's interest came to be the tribunes' *raison d'être*. The negative nature of the tribunes' powers made them particularly well-suited to helping the conservatives, but this weapon was two-edged as Tiberius Gracchus was to show in 133. In that year, two tribunes, one representing the popular view and one the conservative elements in the state, came into head-on collision. This was in theory impossible because, after all, the tribunes were all officers of the people representing their interests, but it was long since they had played this role and these plebeian officers had long been virtually popular magistrates. The argument of Tiberius that M. Octavius was thwarting the people's will and should therefore be deposed has a superficial plausibility, but it ignores the reality of contemporary politics. And this argument would mean that the people, now without even the limited political responsibility of a century earlier, would be free to legislate in accordance with their every whim under the guidance of their chosen leader.

In his year of office Tiberius dealt another blow at the senatorial position. The bequest of his kingdom to the Roman people by Attalus III of Pergamum provided Tiberius with a lucky windfall. His scheme for agrarian reform was in danger of foundering through lack of funds and he now proposed to use part of the legacy to finance it. The Senate, however, reiterated its traditional claims to control finance and provincial and foreign affairs. Tiberius's reply to this claim was to specify in his Bill laid before the *Concilium Plebis* the use to which the money was to be put, and to deny to the Senate their right to settle the affairs of Pergamum. He then went on to propose his continuance in office for a further year, but he had gone too far and it remained for his younger brother Gaius to break down Roman political conventions in this particular way.

The three actions of the Gracchi: the deposition of tribunes opposing the people's will, the immediate re-election of a tribune for any number of years, and the assertion of the right of the people and their leader to interfere in any part of the nation's business—all these were tantamount to a constitutional revolution, a revolution which the people were not fitted to sustain.

This was the situation, exacerbated by the ensuing violence, which faced Sulla forty years later when he sought to restore senatorial control. The Senate suffered extensively at the hands of enterprising tribunes, who had raised up the sovereignty of the people against it. Sulla, so far as we can tell from our imperfect sources, acted to counter such men by making the tribunate a political dead-end and shearing it of all its newer powers, leaving only the *ius auxilii ferendi*, its original power, untouched. The *ius intercessionis*, however, he limited rather than abolished. The tribunate was to disqualify a man from holding any other office and could only be held a second time after an interval of ten years. No ambitious young man would be tempted to rise to power by way of the tribunate and thus it would either disappear through lack of candidates or shelter harmless nonentities. Unfortunately for the

Senate he did not abolish the *Concilium Plebis* which still remained to provide a field in which tribunician power could be reborn.

During the 70's there was vigorous agitation on behalf of the tribunate and in 75 the consul, C. Aurelius Cotta, repealed the law disabling tribunes from holding other office. The tribunes, however, were not able to wring further concessions for themselves from the Senate which had done far more damage to its position by appointing Pompey to a military command in Spain. By this action they allowed him to build up for himself a position from which, although six years below the minimum age and without the necessary quaestorship and praetorship to his name, he could demand and obtain the consulship he wanted. This was in flagrant contravention of the Sullan *lex annalis*.

After the consulship of Pompey and Crassus in 70 the Senate regained control of the situation. For the next three years sound conservatives were elected consul, but in 67 for the first time since Sulla's dictatorship there were among the tribunes two energetic champions of the people, C. Cornelius and A. Gabinius. These men carried out a policy of reform directed against electoral bribery such as had ensured the conservative consuls' election, and against senatorial corruption in dealings with foreign embassies. Gabinius, however, is best known for his *lex de piratis persequendis* under which it was proposed that an extraordinary command should be set up to deal with the piracy which swept the Mediterranean. From the very first Pompey's appointment was widely assumed.

The Senate's reaction was immediate. Q. Lutatius

Catulus and Q. Hortensius, Cicero's great oratorical rival, led the opposition, and two tribunes, L. Roscius Otho and L. Trebellius, were found to support the nobility who alone protested at this badly-needed measure. The clash between M. Octavius and Tiberius Gracchus was re-enacted between Trebellius and Gabinius. Only after violence and having come within an ace of deposition did Trebellius withdraw his veto and allow the bill to be passed.

Pompey's subsequent success was complete, but Rome could not yet rest in the East: the Third Mithridatic War was still dragging on. Confidence in L. Lucullus had been lost and his successors, Q. Marcius Rex and M'. Acilius Glabrio, were utterly incompetent. Pompey was now in the eastern Mediterranean, having brought the pirate war to an end, and the solution must have seemed obvious. With the people's eager support a tribune, C. Manilius, introduced a Bill to hand over the command against Mithridates to Pompey. Catulus and Hortensius again led the opposition of the extreme conservative element in the Senate which still hoped to restore the Sullan constitution. Cicero was joined by Caesar in his support of the Bill and Pompey's recent military achievements could not be denied. In the end the Bill was passed without a struggle.

6. Life of Pompey

Cnaeus Pompeius, the son of Cn. Pompeius Strabo, was born in 106. His father was one of the consuls of 89 and commanded an army in the Social War. The young Pompey saw his first military service under his

father, and in the subsequent Marian domination raised
an army in Picenum on Sulla's behalf. He fought with
such success that he was sent by Sulla to Sicily where
he defeated Carbo, the leader of Marius's supporters on
the island. From there he crossed over to Africa, where
he defeated the Marian remnants. His outstanding
ability was with reluctance recognized by Sulla, who
allowed him, although he was still only an *eques*, to
celebrate a triumph and he was afterwards known by
the title of Magnus. In 77 he helped Catulus defeat
Lepidus, his consular colleague of the previous year,
who had disobeyed the Senate's orders to quit Italy
for his province and was marching on Rome with his
army. When the fighting was over Pompey made
various excuses for not disbanding his army and was
finally granted proconsular *imperium* by an unwilling
Senate to share the command with Metellus Pius
against Sertorius in Spain. Pompey found Sertorius
more than a match for him, and was only able to bring
the war to a successful close after Sertorius·had been
assassinated. He then returned home to enjoy a second
triumph and election as consul for 70 with Crassus as
his colleague. In this year the tribunes regained more
of their lost rights, and in 67 Pompey reaped the
profits. A tribunician measure, the *lex Gabinia*, gave
him his extraordinary command with which to free the
Mediterranean from piracy. This task he accomplished
in three months and in the following year Manilius
proposed the measure supported by Cicero in this
speech.

Manilius's Bill successfully passed, Pompey took over
the command of the war against Mithridates and it was

in the East that he reached the peak of his success. He drove Mithridates from his kingdom, and the enemy who had eluded so many previous generals finally committed suicide. All subsequent organization of the eastern provinces was founded upon Pompey's settlement. He returned to Rome in 61, triumphed over yet another continent and disbanded his army. The Senate, however, persuaded by its more extreme members under the leadership of Cato, refused to grant him land for the settlement of his veterans and the automatic ratification of his *acta* in the East. This refusal threw him into the arms of Caesar and Crassus, who also were at odds with the Senate, and the former saw to it when he became consul in 59 that Pompey obtained what he wanted. In the same year Pompey further cemented the link by marrying Caesar's daughter, Julia.

The key to power at Rome during this period was armed force, and Pompey's lack of it together with his loss of popularity led to the decline of his position. Caesar was building up his army in Gaul and, although Pompey had the important task of supervising the corn-supply for five years, there was no military force attached to his office. His adherence to the so-called Triumvirate wavered, but the bonds were renewed at Luca in 56 and in the following year Pompey and Crassus again shared the consulship. Crassus, realizing that his money-bags were not enough for the rough political struggle now taking place, went off to the East to build up there a military counter-weight to Caesar's Gallic arms. Pompey received Spain as his province for a period of five years and proceeded to govern it by proxy from Rome, to the annoyance of his political opponents who resented his ability to build up an army for himself in Spain while keeping himself in the forefront of political life in the capital.

The violence attending Roman politics grew steadily worse, and in 53 the anarchy which prevented the elections for 52 from being held and the murder of Clodius by Milo led to the appointment of Pompey as sole consul to restore order. He immediately brought forward laws to enable honest elections to be held, and made Metellus Scipio his consular colleague. His wife Julia had died in 54, and he now married Metellus's daughter Cornelia—an outward sign of his steady movement towards reconciliation with the senate. He secured the passage of a law to compel candidates for office to make their announcement in person at Rome, which had the effect of laying Caesar open to attack by his enemies. All ten tribunes, however, joined together to pass a law permitting Caesar to be a candidate for the consulship in his absence. He also destroyed the balance of power between himself and Caesar by arranging that his *imperium* in Spain should be prolonged for a further five years.

In 50 he was put in command of the Republican forces in Italy, and in the following year, fleeing before Caesar's headlong advance down Italy, he crossed over to Greece and set about mobilizing the forces which he should have collected the previous year. Caesar followed him across the Adriatic in 48 but suffered a severe set-back at Dyrrhachium. This, however, was avenged in August at Pharsalus, from which Pompey fled to Egypt where, on 28th September, he was murdered as he stepped ashore.

M. TULLI CICERONIS

DE IMPERIO CN. POMPEI

AD QUIRITES ORATIO

1–3. Cicero is addressing the popular assembly for the first time. Having previously confined his activities to the law courts, he is now ready to speak from the Rostra. He is fortunate that his theme, the merit of Pompey, provides him with an abundance of material.

I. 1. Quamquam mihi semper frequens conspectus vester multo iucundissimus, hic autem locus ad agendum amplissimus, ad dicendum ornatissimus est visus, Quirites, tamen hoc aditu laudis, qui semper optimo cuique maxime patuit, non mea me voluntas adhuc, 5 sed vitae meae rationes ab ineunte aetate susceptae prohibuerunt. Nam cum antea per aetatem nondum huius auctoritatem loci attingere auderem statueremque nihil huc nisi perfectum ingenio, elaboratum industria adferri oportere, omne meum tempus amicorum tem- 10 poribus transmittendum putavi. 2. Ita neque hic locus vacuus umquam fuit ab iis, qui vestram causam defenderent, et meus labor, in privatorum periculis caste integreque versatus, ex vestro iudicio fructum est amplissimum consecutus. Nam cum propter dilationem 15 comitiorum ter praetor primus centuriis cunctis renuntiatus sum, facile intellexi, Quirites, et quid de me iudicaretis et quid aliis praescriberetis. Nunc, cum et auctoritatis in me tantum sit, quantum vos honori-

1

20 bus mandandis esse voluistis, et ad agendum facultatis
tantum, quantum homini vigilanti ex forensi usu
prope cotidiana dicendi exercitatio potuit adferre, certe
et si quid auctoritatis in me est, apud eos utar, qui
eam mihi dederunt, et si quid in dicendo consequi
25 possum, iis ostendam potissimum, qui ei quoque rei
fructum suo iudicio tribuendum esse duxerunt. 3. Atque
illud in primis mihi laetandum iure esse video, quod
in hac insolita mihi ex hoc loco ratione dicendi causa
talis oblata est, in qua oratio deesse nemini possit.
30 Dicendum est enim de Cn. Pompei singulari eximiaque
virtute: huius autem orationis difficilius est exitum
quam principium invenire. Ita mihi non tam copia
quam modus in dicendo quaerendus est.

4–5. *A dangerous war is being fought in Asia by Mithridates and*
Tigranes against Rome and her allies. The Roman generals
have failed to deal with the situation and all men are demanding
that Pompey be appointed commander-in-chief.

II. 4. Atque ut inde oratio mea proficiscatur, unde
haec omnis causa ducitur, bellum grave et periculosum
vestris vectigalibus ac sociis a duobus potentissimis
regibus infertur, Mithridate et Tigrane, quorum alter
5 relictus, alter lacessitus occasionem sibi ad occupandam
Asiam oblatam esse arbitrantur. Equitibus Romanis,
honestissimis viris, adferuntur ex Asia cotidie litterae,
quorum magnae res aguntur, in vestris vectigalibus
exercendis occupatae; qui ad me pro necessitudine,
10 quae mihi est cum illo ordine, causam rei publicae
periculaque rerum suarum detulerunt: 5. Bithyniae,
quae nunc vestra provincia est, vicos exustos esse complures: regnum Ariobarzanis, quod finitimum est ves-

tris vectigalibus, totum esse in hostium potestate; L. Lucullum magnis rebus gestis ab eo bello discedere; 15 huic qui successerit non satis esse paratum ad tantum bellum administrandum; unum ab omnibus sociis et civibus ad id bellum imperatorem deposci atque expeti, eundem hunc unum ab hostibus metui, praeterea neminem. 20

6. *The nature of the war and the importance of the interests at stake.*

6. Causa quae sit videtis: nunc quid agendum sit considerate. Primum mihi videtur de genere belli, deinde de magnitudine, tum de imperatore deligendo esse dicendum. Genus est belli eius modi, quod maxime vestros animos excitare atque inflammare ad 5 persequendi studium debeat: in quo agitur populi Romani gloria, quae vobis a maioribus cum magna in omnibus rebus, tum summa in re militari tradita est; agitur salus sociorum atque amicorum, pro qua multa maiores vestri magna et gravia bella gesserunt; aguntur 10 certissima populi Romani vectigalia et maxima, quibus amissis et pacis ornamenta et subsidia belli requiretis; aguntur bona multorum civium, quibus est a vobis et ipsorum et rei publicae causa consulendum.

7–8. *The massacre of Roman citizens in the First Mithridatic War has still to be avenged because, in spite of the triumphs which have been celebrated over Mithridates, he is still king.*

III. 7. Et quoniam semper appetentes gloriae praeter ceteras gentes atque avidi laudis fuistis, delenda est vobis illa macula Mithridatico bello superiore concepta,

quae penitus iam insedit ac nimis inveteravit in populi
5 Romani nomine, quod is, qui uno die tota in Asia, tot
in civitatibus, uno nuntio atque una significatione
litterarum cives Romanos necandos trucidandosque
denotavit, non modo adhuc poenam nullam suo dignam
scelere suscepit, sed ab illo tempore annum iam tertium
10 et vicesimum regnat, et ita regnat, ut se non Ponti
neque Cappadociae latebris occultare velit, sed emergere ex patrio regno atque in vestris vectigalibus, hoc
est in Asiae luce versari.   8. Etenim adhuc ita nostri
cum illo rege contenderunt imperatores, ut ab illo
15 insignia victoriae, non victoriam reportarent. Triumphavit L. Sulla, triumphavit L. Murena de Mithridate,
duo fortissimi viri et summi imperatores, sed ita
triumpharunt, ut ille pulsus superatusque regnaret.
Verum tamen illis imperatoribus laus est tribuenda,
20 quod egerunt, venia danda, quod reliquerunt, propterea
quod ab eo bello Sullam in Italiam res publica,
Murenam Sulla revocavit.

*9–11. Mithridates has been preparing to renew the struggle and
negotiating with Sertorius in Spain. The latter has been
crushed by Pompey, and at first Lucullus fought with success
against Mithridates.*

IV. 9. Mithridates autem omne reliquum tempus non
ad oblivionem veteris belli, sed ad comparationem novi
contulit: qui postea, cum maximas aedificasset ornassetque classes exercitusque permagnos quibuscumque
5 ex gentibus potuisset comparasset et se Bosporanis,
finitimis suis, bellum inferre simularet, usque in Hispaniam legatos ac litteras misit ad eos duces, quibus-
cum tum bellum gerebamus, ut, cum duobus in locis

disiunctissimis maximeque diversis uno consilio a binis
hostium copiis bellum terra marique gereretur, vos 10
ancipiti contentione districti de imperio. dimicaretis.
10. Sed tamen alterius partis periculum, Sertorianae
atque Hispaniensis, quae multo plus firmamenti ac
roboris habebat, Cn. Pompei divino consilio ac singulari
virtute depulsum est: in altera parte ita res a L. Lucullo, 15
summo viro, est administrata, ut initia illa rerum
gestarum magna atque praeclara non felicitati eius,
sed virtuti, haec autem extrema, quae nuper acciderunt,
non culpae, sed fortunae tribuenda esse videantur.
Sed de Lucullo dicam alio loco, et ita dicam, Quirites, 20
ut neque vera laus ei detracta oratione mea neque
falsa adficta esse videatur: 11. de vestri imperii
dignitate atque gloria, quoniam is est exorsus orationis
meae, videte quem vobis animum suscipiendum putetis.

*11–13. The Romans' forefathers would not have tolerated such
outrages as are being inflicted by Mithridates. In their desperate position the allies wish Rome to send Pompey.*

V. Maiores nostri saepe, mercatoribus aut naviculariis nostris iniuriosius tractatis, bella gesserunt; vos,
tot milibus civium Romanorum uno nuntio atque uno
tempore necatis, quo tandem animo esse debetis? Legati
quod erant appellati superbius, Corinthum patres 5
vestri, totius Graeciae lumen, exstinctum esse voluerunt: vos eum regem inultum esse patiemini, qui
legatum populi Romani consularem vinculis ac verberi-
bus atque omni supplicio excruciatum necavit? Illi
libertatem civium Romanorum imminutam non tule- 10
runt: vos vitam ereptam neglegetis? ius legationis
verbo violatum illi persecuti sunt: vos legatum omni

supplicio interfectum relinquetis? 12. Videte ne, ut
illis pulcherrimum fuit tantam vobis imperii gloriam
15 tradere, sic vobis turpissimum sit id quod accepistis
tueri et conservare non posse.

Quid? quod salus sociorum summum in periculum
ac discrimen vocatur, quo tandem animo ferre debetis?
Regno est expulsus Ariobarzanes rex, socius populi
20 Romani atque amicus; imminent duo reges toti Asiae,
non solum vobis inimicissimi, sed etiam vestris sociis
atque amicis; civitates autem omnes cuncta Asia atque Graecia vestrum auxilium exspectare propter periculi magnitudinem coguntur; imperatorem a vobis
25 certum deposcere, cum praesertim vos alium miseritis,
neque audent neque se id facere sine summo periculo
posse arbitrantur. 13. Vident et sentiunt hoc idem
quod vos, unum virum esse, in quo summa sint omnia,
et eum propter esse, quo etiam carent aegrius: cuius
30 adventu ipso atque nomine, tametsi ille ad maritimum
bellum venerit, tamen impetus hostium repressos esse
intellegunt ac retardatos. Hi vos, quoniam libere
loqui non licet, taciti rogant, ut se quoque, sicut
ceterarum provinciarum socios, dignos existimetis
35 quorum salutem tali viro commendetis, atque hoc
etiam magis, quod ceteros in provinciam eius modi
homines cum imperio mittimus, ut, etiam si ab hoste
defendant, tamen ipsorum adventus in urbes sociorum
non multum ab hostili expugnatione differant: hunc
40 audiebant antea, nunc praesentem vident tanta temperantia, tanta mansuetudine, tanta humanitate, ut ii
beatissimi esse videantur, apud quos ille diutissime
commoretur.

14–16. Asia's revenues are greater than those of any other country, and must be defended not only from capture by Mithridates but from the fear of war; for the mere prospect of invasion may mean the loss of a year's income.

VI. 14. Quare, si propter socios, nulla ipsi iniuria lacessiti, maiores nostri cum Antiocho, cum Philippo, cum Aetolis, cum Poenis bella gesserunt, quanto vos studiosius convenit, iniuriis provocatos, sociorum salutem una cum imperii vestri dignitate defendere, prae- 5 sertim cum de maximis vestris vectigalibus agatur? Nam ceterarum provinciarum vectigalia, Quirites, tanta sunt, ut iis ad ipsas provincias tuendas vix contenti esse possimus: Asia vero tam opima est ac fertilis, ut et ubertate agrorum et varietate fructuum et magni- 10 tudine pastionis et multitudine earum rerum, quae exportantur, facile omnibus terris antecellat. Itaque haec vobis provincia, Quirites, si et belli utilitatem et pacis dignitatem retinere vultis, non modo a calamitate, sed etiam a metu calamitatis est defendenda. 15 15. Nam in ceteris rebus, cum venit calamitas, tum detrimentum accipitur: at in vectigalibus non solum adventus mali, sed etiam metus ipse adfert calamitatem. Nam cum hostium copiae non longe absunt, etiam si inruptio nulla facta est, tamen pecua relinquuntur, agri 20 cultura deseritur, mercatorum navigatio conquiescit. Ita neque ex portu neque ex decumis neque ex scriptura vectigal conservari potest; quare saepe totius anni fructus una rumore periculi atque uno belli terrore amittitur. 16. Quo tandem igitur animo esse 25 existimatis aut eos, qui vectigalia nobis pensitant, aut eos, qui exercent atque exigunt, cum duo reges cum maximis copiis propter adsint? cum una excursio equi-

tatus perbrevi tempore totius anni vectigal auferre
30 possit? cum publicani familias maximas, quas in saltibus
habent, quas in agris, quas in portibus atque custodiis,
magno periculo se habere arbitrentur? Putatisne vos
illis rebus frui posse, nisi eos, qui vobis fructui sunt,
conservaritis, non solum, ut ante dixi, calamitate, sed
35 etiam calamitatis formidine liberatos?

*17–19. The war might also ruin the men who farm the province's
taxes and others who have financial interests in Asia. This
would bring about a collapse of credit at Rome, and a financial
crisis at home as well as in the province.*

VII. 17. Ac ne illud quidem vobis neglegendum est,
quod mihi ego extremum proposueram, cum essem de
belli genere dicturus, quod ad multorum bona civium
Romanorum pertinet: quorum vobis pro vestra sapi-
5 entia, Quirites, habenda est ratio diligenter. Nam et
publicani, homines honestissimi atque ornatissimi, suas
rationes et copias in illam provinciam contulerunt,
quorum ipsorum per se res et fortunae vobis curae esse
debent; etenim si vectigalia nervos esse rei publicae
10 semper duximus, eum certe ordinem, qui exercet illa,
firmamentum ceterorum ordinum recte esse dicemus.
18. Deinde ex ceteris ordinibus homines gnavi atque
industrii partim ipsi in Asia negotiantur, quibus vos
absentibus consulere debetis, partim eorum in ea
15 provincia pecunías magnas collocatas habent. Est
igitur humanitatis vestrae magnum numerum eorum
civium calamitate prohibere, sapientiae videre, multorum civium calamitatem a re publica seiunctam esse
non posse. Etenim primum illud parvi refert, nos
20 publicanis amissa vectigalia postea victoria recuperare,

neque enim isdem redimendi facultas erit propter calamitatem neque aliis voluntas propter timorem. 19. Deinde, quod nos eadem Asia atque idem iste Mithridates initio belli Asiatici docuit, id quidem certe calamitate docti memoria retinere debemus. Nam 25 tum, cum in Asia res magnas permulti amiserant, scimus Romae solutione impedita fidem concidisse. Non enim possunt una in civitate multi rem ac fortunas amittere, ut non plures secum in eandem trahant calamitatem. A quo periculo prohibete rem publicam, 30 et mihi credite, id quod ipsi videtis: haec fides atque haec ratio pecuniarum, quae Romae, quae in foro versatur, implicata est cum illis pecuniis Asiaticis et cohaeret; ruere illa non possunt, ut haec non eodem labefacta motu concidant. Quare videte num dubitan- 35 dum vobis sit omni studio ad id bellum incumbere, in quo gloria nominis vestri, salus sociorum, vectigalia maxima, fortunae plurimorum civium coniunctae cum re publica defendantur.

20–21. *The dimensions of the war have been greatly reduced by Lucullus, whose achievements Cicero readily recognizes.*

VIII. 20. Quoniam de genere belli dixi, nunc de magnitudine pauca dicam. Potest enim hoc dici, belli genus esse ita necessarium, ut sit gerendum, non esse ita magnum, ut sit pertimescendum. In quo maxime laborandum est, ne forte ea vobis, quae diligentissime 5 providenda sunt, contemnenda esse videantur. Atque ut omnes intellegant me L. Lucullo tantum impertire laudis, quantum forti viro et sapienti homini et magno imperatori debeatur, dico eius adventu maximas

10 Mithridati copias omnibus rebus ornatas atque instructas fuisse urbemque Asiae clarissimam nobisque
amicissimam, Cyzicenorum, obsessam esse ab ipso rege
maxima multitudine et oppugnatam vehementissime,
quam L. Lucullus virtute, assiduitate, consilio summis
15 obsidionis periculis liberavit: 21. ab eodem imperatore
classem magnam et ornatam, quae ducibus Sertorianis
ad Italiam studio atque odio inflammata raperetur,
superatam esse atque depressam; magnas hostium
praeterea copias multis proeliis esse deletas patefactum-
20 que nostris legionibus esse Pontum, qui antea populo
Romano ex omni aditu clausus fuisset; Sinopen atque
Amisum, quibus in oppidis erant domicilia regis omnibus
rebus ornata ac referta, ceterasque urbes Ponti et Cappadociae permultas uno aditu adventuque esse captas;
25 regem spoliatum regno patrio atque avito ad alios se
reges atque ad alias gentes supplicem contulisse: atque
haec omnia salvis populi Romani sociis atque integris
vectigalibus esse gesta. Satis opinor hoc esse laudis,
atque ita, Quirites, ut hoc vos intellegatis, a nullo
30 istorum, qui huic obtrectant legi atque causae, L. Lucullum similiter ex hoc loco esse laudatum.

22–26. *In his flight Mithridates left behind his treasure and by
this stratagem escaped the pursuing Roman troops. He raised
other peoples against Rome and in defeat rallied round him
more allies than had joined him in his days of victory. A
Roman army, anxious only to return from those distant regions,
was heavily defeated and the general, Lucullus, was ordered to
disband part of his army and hand over part to his successor
Glabrio.*

IX. 22. Requiretur fortasse nunc, quem ad modum,
cum haec ita sint, reliquum possit magnum esse bellum.

Cognoscite, Quirites; non enim hoc sine causa quaeri
videtur. Primum ex suo regno sic Mithridates pro-
fugit, ut ex eodem Ponto Medea illa quondam profu- 5
gisse dicitur, quam praedicant in fuga fratris sui
membra in iis locis, qua se parens persequeretur, dis-
sipavisse, ut eorum collectio dispersa maerorque patrius
celeritatem persequendi retardaret. Sic Mithridates
fugiens maximam vim auri atque argenti pulcherrima- 10
rumque rerum omnium, quas et a maioribus acceperat
et ipse bello superiore ex tota Asia direptas in suum
regnum congesserat, in Ponto omnem reliquit. Haec
dum nostri colligunt omnia diligentius, rex ipse e
manibus effugit. Ita illum in persequendi studio 15
maeror, hos laetitia tardavit. 23. Hunc in illo timore
et fuga Tigranes, rex Armenius, excepit diffidentemque
rebus suis confirmavit et adflictum erexit perditumque
recreavit. Cuius in regnum posteaquam L. Lucullus
cum exercitu venit, plures etiam gentes contra impera- 20
torem nostrum concitatae sunt. Erat enim metus
iniectus iis nationibus, quas numquam populus Romanus neque lacessendas bello neque temptandas putavit: erat etiam alia gravis atque vehemens opinio,
quae per animos gentium barbararum pervaserat, fani 25
locupletissimi et religiosissimi diripiendi causa in eas
oras nostrum esse exercitum adductum. Ita nationes
multae atque magnae novo quodam terrore ac metu
concitabantur. Noster autem exercitus tametsi urbem
ex Tigrani regno ceperat et proeliis usus erat secun- 30
dis, tamen nimia longinquitate locorum ac desiderio
suorum commovebatur. 24. Hic iam plura non dicam;
fuit enim illud extremum, ut ex iis locis a militibus
nostris reditus magis maturus quam progressio longior

35 quaereretur. Mithridates autem et suam manum iam
confirmarat, et magnis adventiciis auxiliis multorum
regum et nationum iuvabatur. Nam hoc fere sic fieri
solere accepimus, ut regum adflictae fortunae facile
multorum opes adliciant ad misericordiam maximeque
40 eorum, qui aut reges sunt aut vivunt in regno, ut iis
nomen regale magnum et sanctum esse videatur. 25.
Itaque tantum victus efficere potuit, quantum incolumis
numquam est ausus optare. Nam cum se in regnum
suum recepisset, non fuit eo contentus, quod ei praeter
45 spem acciderat, ut illam, posteaquam pulsus erat,
terram umquam attingeret, sed in exercitum nostrum
clarum atque victorem impetum fecit. Sinite hoc loco,
Quirites, sicut poetae solent, qui res Romanas scribunt,
praeterire me nostram calamitatem, quae tanta fuit, ut
50 eam ad aures imperatoris non ex proelio nuntius, sed ex
sermone rumor adferret. 26. Hic in illo ipso malo
gravissimaque belli offensione L. Lucullus, qui tamen
aliqua ex parte iis incommodis mederi fortasse potuisset,
vestro iussu coactus, quod imperii diuturnitati modum
55 statuendum vetere exemplo putavistis, partem militum,
qui iam stipendiis confectis erant, dimisit, partem M'.
Glabrioni tradidit. Multa praetereo consulto, sed ea
vos coniectura perspicite, quantum illud bellum factum
putetis, quod coniungant reges potentissimi, renovent
60 agitatae nationes, suscipiant integrae gentes, novus
imperator noster accipiat vetere exercitu pulso.

27–28. Pompey alone is qualified for the command in such a
war. He has the experience, ability, prestige, and good fortune.

X. 27. Satis mihi multa verba fecisse videor, quare
esset hoc bellum genere ipso necessarium, magnitudine

periculosum: restat ut de imperatore ad id bellum
deligendo ac tantis rebus praeficiendo dicendum esse
videatur. Utinam, Quirites, virorum fortium atque 5
innocentium copiam tantam haberetis, ut haec vobis
deliberatio difficilis esset, quemnam potissimum tantis
rebus ac tanto bello praeficiendum putaretis! nunc
vero cum sit unus Cn. Pompeius, qui non modo eorum
hominum, qui nunc sunt, gloriam, sed etiam antiqui- 10
tatis memoriam virtute superarit, quae res est quae
cuiusquam animum in hac causa dubium facere
possit? 28. Ego enim sic existimo, in summo imperatore
quattuor has res inesse oportere: scientiam rei militaris,
virtutem, auctoritatem, felicitatem. Quis igitur hoc 15
homine scientior umquam aut fuit aut esse debuit?
qui e ludo atque pueritiae disciplinis, bello maximo atque
acerrimis hostibus, ad patris exercitum atque in militiae
disciplinam profectus est; qui extrema pueritia miles
in exercitu fuit summi imperatoris, ineunte adules- 20
centia maximi ipse exercitus imperator; qui saepius
cum hoste conflixit quam quisquam cum inimico concertavit, plura bella gessit quam ceteri legerunt, plures
provincias confecit quam alii concupiverunt; cuius
adulescentia ad scientiam rei militaris non alienis 25
praeceptis sed suis imperiis, non offensionibus belli sed
victoriis, non stipendiis sed triumphis est erudita.
Quod denique genus esse belli potest, in quo illum non
exercuerit fortuna rei publicae? Civile, Africanum,
Transalpinum, Hispaniense, servile, navale bellum, varia 30
et diversa genera et bellorum et hostium, non solum
gesta ab hoc uno, sed etiam confecta nullam rem esse
declarant in usu positam militari, quae huius viri
scientiam fugere possit.

29–30. *The military ability of Pompey is outstanding, as is shown by his achievements in Italy, Sicily, Africa, Gaul, Spain, and Italy.*

XI. 29. Iam vero virtuti Cn. Pompei quae potest oratio par inveniri? quid est quod quisquam aut illo dignum aut vobis novum aut cuiquam inauditum possit adferre? Neque enim illae sunt solae virtutes impe-
5 ratoriae, quae vulgo existimantur, labor in negotiis, fortitudo in periculis, industria in agendo, celeritas in conficiendo, consilium in providendo, quae tanta sunt in hoc uno, quanta in omnibus reliquis imperatoribus, quos aut vidimus aut audivimus, non fuerunt. 30.
10 Testis est Italia, quam ille ipse victor L. Sulla huius virtute et subsidio confessus est liberatam: testis est Sicilia, quam multis undique cinctam periculis non terrore belli, sed consilii celeritate explicavit: testis est Africa, quae magnis oppressa hostium copiis eorum ipsorum
15 sanguine redundavit: testis est Gallia, per quam legionibus nostris iter in Hispaniam Gallorum internicione patefactum est: testis est Hispania, quae saepissime plurimos hostes ab hoc superatos prostratosque conspexit: testis est iterum et saepius Italia,
20 quae cum servili bello taetro periculosoque premeretur, ab hoc auxilium absente expetivit, quod bellum exspectatione eius attenuatum atque imminutum est, adventu sublatum ac sepultum.

31–35. *The menace of the pirates used to spread over the whole Mediterranean. Rome's allies were often in their hands and the very coasts and highways of Italy were not free from their attacks. Yet in less than a year these pirates were crushed by Pompey.*

31. Testes nunc vero iam omnes orae atque omnes exterae gentes ac nationes, denique maria omnia, cum universa, tum in singulis oris omnes sinus atque portus. Quis enim toto mari locus per hos annos aut tam firmum habuit praesidium, ut tutus esset, aut tam fuit 5 abditus, ut lateret? Quis navigavit, qui non se aut mortis aut servitutis periculo committeret, cum aut hieme aut referto praedonum mari navigaret? Hoc tantum bellum, tam turpe, tam vetus, tam late divisum atque dispersum quis umquam arbitraretur aut ab 10 omnibus imperatoribus uno anno aut omnibus annis ab uno imperatore confici posse? 32. Quam provinciam tenuistis a praedonibus liberam per hosce annos? quod vectigal vobis tutum fuit? quem socium defendistis? cui praesidio classibus vestris fuistis? Quam multas 15 existimatis insulas esse desertas, quam multas aut metu relictas aut a praedonibus captas urbes esse sociorum? XII. Sed quid ego longinqua commemoro? Fuit hoc quondam, fuit proprium populi Romani, longe a domo bellare et propugnaculis imperii sociorum fortunas, non 20 sua tecta defendere. Sociis ego nostris mare per hosce annos clausum fuisse dicam, cum exercitus vestri numquam Brundisio nisi hieme summa transmiserint? Qui ad vos ab exteris nationibus venirent, captos querar, cum legati populi Romani redempti sint? 25 mercatoribus tutum mare non fuisse dicam, cum duodecim secures in praedonum potestatem per-venerint? 33. Cnidum aut Colophonem aut Samum, nobilissimas urbes, innumerabilesque alias captas esse commemorem, cum vestros portus atque eos portus, 30 quibus vitam et spiritum ducitis, in praedonum fuisse potestate sciatis? An vero ignoratis portum Caietae

celeberrimum ac plenissimum navium inspectante
praetore a praedonibus esse direptum? ex Miseno
35 autem eius ipsius liberos, qui cum praedonibus antea
bellum gesserat, a praedonibus esse sublatos? Nam
quid ego Ostiense incommodum atque illam labem atque ignominiam rei publicae querar, cum prope inspectantibus vobis classis ea, cui consul populi Romani
40 praepositus esset, a praedonibus capta atque oppressa
est? Pro di immortales! tantamne unius hominis
incredibilis ac divina virtus tam brevi tempore lucem
adferre rei publicae potuit, ut vos, qui modo ante
ostium Tiberinum classem hostium videbatis, nunc
45 nullam intra Oceani ostium praedonum navem esse
audiatis? 34. Atque haec qua celeritate gesta sint,
quamquam videtis, tamen a me in dicendo praetereunda
non sunt. Quis enim umquam aut obeundi negotii aut
consequendi quaestus studio tam brevi tempore tot
50 loca adire, tantos cursus conficere potuit, quam celeriter
Cn. Pompeio duce tanti belli impetus navigavit? qui
nondum tempestivo ad navigandum mari Siciliam adiit,
Africam exploravit, in Sardiniam cum classe venit,
atque haec tria frumentaria subsidia rei publicae
55 firmissimis praesidiis classibusque munivit. 35. Inde
cum se in Italiam recepisset, duabus Hispaniis et Gallia
Transalpina praesidiis ac navibus confirmata, missis
item in oram Illyrici maris et in Achaiam omnemque
Graeciam navibus Italiae duo maria maximis classibus
60 firmissimisque praesidiis adornavit, ipse autem, ut
Brundisio profectus est, undequinquagesimo die totam
ad imperium populi Romani Ciliciam adiunxit: omnes,
qui ubique praedones fuerunt, partim capti interfecti-
que sunt, partim unius huius se imperio ac potestati

dediderunt. Idem Cretensibus, cum ad eum usque in 65
Pamphyliam legatos deprecatoresque misissent, spem
deditionis non ademit obsidesque imperavit. Ita tantum bellum, tam diuturnum, tam longe lateque dispersum, quo bello omnes gentes ac nationes premeban-
tur, Cn. Pompeius extrema hieme apparavit, ineunte 70
vere suscepit, media aestate confecit.

36. *The qualities needed by a first-class general include—in*
addition to military ability—integrity, self-control, honour,
courtesy, and intellect.

XIII. 36. Est haec divina atque incredibilis virtus
imperatoris: quid? ceterae, quas paulo ante commemorare coeperam, quantae atque quam multae sunt!
Non enim bellandi virtus solum in summo ac perfecto
imperatore quaerenda est, sed multae sunt artes 5
eximiae huius administrae comitesque virtutis. Ac
primum quanta innocentia debent esse imperatores!
quanta deinde in omnibus rebus temperantia! quanta
fide, quanta facilitate, quanto ingenio, quanta humanitate! quae breviter qualia sint in Cn. Pompeio con- 10
sideremus; summa enim omnia sunt, Quirites, sed ea
magis ex aliorum contentione quam ipsa per sese
cognosci atque intellegi possunt.

37-39. *The superiority of Pompey to certain other generals,*
who were corrupt and whose armies were more feared than those
of the enemy, is noted. Pompey never allowed his army to
commit excesses.

37. Quem enim imperatorem possumus ullo in numero
putare, cuius in exercitu centuriatus veneant atque

venierint? quid hunc hominem magnum aut amplum
de re publica cogitare, qui pecuniam ex aerario de-
5 promptam ad bellum administrandum aut propter
cupiditatem provinciae magistratibus diviserit aut
propter avaritiam Romae in quaestu reliquerit? Vestra
admurmuratio facit, Quirites, ut agnoscere videamini,
qui haec fecerint: ego autem nomino neminem; quare
10 irasci mihi nemo poterit, nisi qui ante de se voluerit
confiteri. Itaque propter hanc avaritiam imperatorum
quantas calamitates, quocumque ventum est, nostri
exercitus ferant, quis ignorat? 38. Itinera, quae per
hosce annos in Italia per agros atque oppida civium
15 Romanorum nostri imperatores fecerint, recordamini:
tum facilius statuetis, quid apud exteras nationes fieri
existimetis. Utrum plures arbitramini per hosce annos
militum vestrorum armis hostium urbes an hibernis
sociorum civitates esse deletas? Neque enim potest
20 exercitum is continere imperator, qui se ipse non
continet, neque severus esse in iudicando, qui alios in se
severos esse iudices non vult. 39. Hic miramur hunc
hominem tantum excellere ceteris, cuius legiones sic in
Asiam pervenerint, ut non modo manus tanti exercitus,
25 sed ne vestigium quidem cuiquam pacato nocuisse
dicatur? Iam vero quem ad modum milites hibernent,
cotidie sermones ac litterae perferuntur. Non modo ut
sumptum faciat in militem nemini vis adfertur, sed ne
cupienti quidem cuiquam permittitur. Hiemis enim,
30 non avaritiae perfugium maiores nostri in sociorum
atque amicorum tectis esse voluerunt.

*40–42. In other ways Pompey has shown self-control and has
restored Rome's earlier reputation for moderation. His qualities
make him the man best suited to finish this war.*

XIV. 40. Age vero ceteris in rebus qua ille sit
temperantia, considerate: Unde illam tantam celeritatem et tam incredibilem cursum inventum putatis?
Non enim illum eximia vis remigum aut ars inaudita
quaedam gubernandi aut venti aliqui novi tam celeriter 5
in ultimas terras pertulerunt, sed eae res, quae ceteros
remorari solent, non retardarunt: non avaritia ab
instituto cursu ad praedam aliquam devocavit, non
libido ad voluptatem, non amoenitas ad delectationem,
non nobilitas urbis ad cognitionem, non denique 10
labor ipse ad quietem; postremo signa et tabulas
ceteraque ornamenta Graecorum oppidorum, quae
ceteri tollenda esse arbitrantur, ea sibi ille ne visenda
quidem existimavit. 41. Itaque omnes nunc in iis locis
Cn. Pompeium sicut aliquem non ex hac urbe missum, 15
sed de caelo delapsum intuentur; nunc denique
incipiunt credere, fuisse homines Romanos hac quondam continentia, quod iam nationibus exteris incredibile ac falso memoriae proditum videbatur; nunc
imperii vestri splendor illis gentibus lucem adferre 20
coepit; nunc intellegunt non sine causa maiores suos
tum, cum ea temperantia magistratus habebamus,
servire populo Romano quam imperare aliis maluisse.
Iam vero ita faciles aditus ad eum privatorum, ita
liberae querimoniae de aliorum iniuriis esse dicuntur, 25
ut is qui dignitate principibus excellit, facilitate infimis
par esse videatur. 42. Iam quantum consilio, quantum
dicendi gravitate et copia valeat, in quo ipso inest
quaedam dignitas imperatoria, vos, Quirites, hoc ipso
ex loco saepe cognovistis. Fidem vero eius quantam 30
inter socios existimari putatis, quam hostes omnes
omnium generum sanctissimam iudicarint? Humani-

tate iam tanta est, ut difficile dictu sit, utrum hostes
magis virtutem eius pugnantes timuerint an man-
35 suetudinem victi dilexerint. Et quisquam dubitabit
quin huic hoc tantum bellum permittendum sit, qui
ad omnia nostrae memoriae bella conficienda divino
quodam consilio natus esse videatur?

*43–45. The prestige of Pompey is most important. The whole
world knows how greatly he is honoured at Rome, and the mere
news of his arrival restrained Mithridates and Tigranes after
their victory.*

XV. 43. Et quoniam auctoritas quoque in bellis
administrandis multum atque in imperio militari valet,
certe nemini dubium est quin ea re idem ille imperator
plurimum possit. Vehementer autem pertinere ad
5 bella administranda, quid hostes, quid socii de imperatoribus nostris existiment, quis ignorat, cum scia-
mus homines in tantis rebus, ut aut contemnant aut
metuant, aut oderint aut ament, opinione non minus
et fama quam aliqua ratione certa commoveri? Quod
10 igitur nomen umquam in orbe terrarum clarius fuit?
cuius res gestae pares? de quo homine vos, id quod
maxime facit auctoritatem, tanta et tam praeclara
iudicia fecistis? 44. An vero ullam usquam esse oram
tam desertam putatis, quo non illius diei fama perva-
15 serit, cum universus populus Romanus referto foro com-
pletisque omnibus templis, ex quibus hic locus conspici
potest, unum sibi ad commune omnium gentium bellum
Cn. Pompeium imperatorem depoposcit? Itaque, ut
plura non dicam neque aliorum exemplis confirmem,
20 quantum auctoritas valeat in bello, ab eodem Cn
Pompeio omnium rerum egregiarum exempla sumantur:

qui quo die a vobis maritimo bello praepositus est
imperator, tanta repente vilitas annonae ex summa
inopia et caritate rei frumentariae consecuta est unius
hominis spe ac nomine, quantum vix in summa uber- 25
tate agrorum diuturna pax efficere potuisset. 45. Iam
accepta in Ponto calamitate ex eo proelio, de quo vos
paulo ante invitus admonui, cum socii pertimuissent,
hostium opes animique crevissent, satis firmum praesidium provincia non haberet, amisissetis Asiam, 30
Quirites, nisi ad ipsum discrimen eius temporis divinitus
Cn. Pompeium ad eas regiones fortuna populi Romani
attulisset.   Huius adventus et Mithridatem insolita
inflatum victoria continuit et Tigranem magnis copiis
minitantem Asiae retardavit.   Et quisquam dubitabit, 35
quid virtute perfecturus sit, qui tantum auctoritate
perfecerit? aut quam facile imperio atque exercitu
socios et vectigalia conservaturus sit, qui ipso nomine
ac rumore defenderit?

46. *Rome's enemies show by their behaviour how highly they
think of Pompey.*

XVI. 46. Age vero illa res quantam declarat eiusdem
hominis apud hostes populi Romani auctoritatem, quod
ex locis tam longinquis tamque diversis tam brevi
tempore omnes huic se uni dediderunt: quod a communi
Cretensium legati, cum in eorum insula noster imperator 5
exercitusque esset, ad Cn. Pompeium in ultimas prope
terras venerunt eique se omnes Cretensium civitates
dedere velle dixerunt! Quid? idem iste Mithridates
nonne ad eundem Cn. Pompeium legatum usque in
Hispaniam misit? eum quem Pompeius legatum 10

semper iudicavit, ii, quibus erat molestum ad eum potissimum esse missum, speculatorem quam legatum iudicari maluerunt. Potestis igitur iam constituere, Quirites, hanc auctoritatem, multis postea rebus gestis 15 magnisque vestris iudiciis amplificatam, quantum apud illos reges, quantum apud exteras nationes valituram esse existimetis.

47–48. The good fortune of Pompey is outstanding and he has enjoyed more than anybody could dare to desire for himself.

47. Reliquum est ut de felicitate, quam praestare de se ipso nemo potest, meminisse et commemorare de altero possumus, sicut aequum est homines de potestate deorum, timide et pauca dicamus. Ego enim sic 5 existimo, Maximo, Marcello, Scipioni, Mario et ceteris magnis imperatoribus non solum propter virtutem, sed etiam propter fortunam saepius imperia mandata atque exercitus esse commissos. Fuit enim profecto quibusdam summis viris quaedam ad amplitudinem et ad 10 gloriam et ad res magnas bene gerendas divinitus adiuncta fortuna. De huius autem hominis felicitate, de quo nunc agimus, hac utar moderatione dicendi, non ut in illius potestate fortunam positam esse dicam, sed ut praeterita meminisse, reliqua sperare videamur, 15 ne aut invisa dis· immortalibus oratio nostra aut ingrata esse videatur. 48. Itaque non sum praedicaturus, quantas ille res domi militiae, terra marique, quantaque felicitate gesserit, ut eius semper voluntatibus non modo cives adsenserint, socii obtemperarint, hostes 20 oboedierint, sed etiam venti tempestatesque obsecundarint: hoc brevissime dicam, neminem umquam tam impudentem fuisse, qui ab dis immortalibus tot et

tantas res tacitus auderet optare, quot et quantas di
immortales ad Cn. Pompeium detulerunt: quod ut illi
proprium ac perpetuum sit, Quirites, cum communis 25
salutis atque imperii, tum ipsius hominis causa, sicuti
facitis, velle et optare debetis.

*49–50. For these reasons, and because he is close at hand, Rome
must appoint Pompey to the command.*

49. Quare cum et bellum sit ita necessarium, ut
neglegi non possit, ita magnum, ut accuratissime sit
administrandum, et cum ei imperatorem praeficere
possitis, in quo sit eximia belli scientia, singularis virtus,
clarissima auctoritas, egregia fortuna, dubitatis, 5
Quirites, quin hoc tantum boni, quod vobis ab dis
immortalibus oblatum et datum est, in rem publicam
conservandam atque amplificandam conferatis? XVII.
50. Quodsi Romae Cn. Pompeius privatus esset hoc
tempore, tamen ad tantum bellum is erat deligendus 10
atque mittendus: nunc, cum ad ceteras summas utili-
tates haec quoque opportunitas adiungatur, ut in iis
ipsis locis adsit, ut habeat exercitum, ut ab iis qui
habent accipere statim possit, quid exspectamus? aut
cur non ducibus dis immortalibus eidem, cui cetera 15
summa cum salute rei publicae commissa sunt, hoc
quoque bellum regium committamus?

*51. Catulus and Hortensius, men of high standing, oppose this
view.*

51. At enim vir clarissimus, amantissimus rei publicae, vestris beneficiis amplissimis adfectus, Q. Catulus,
itemque summis ornamentis honoris, fortunae, virtutis,

ingenii praeditus, Q. Hortensius, ab hac ratione dis-
5 sentiunt: quorum ego auctoritatem apud vos multis
locis plurimum valuisse et valere oportere confiteor,
sed in hac causa, tametsi cognoscetis auctoritates con-
trarias virorum fortissimorum et clarissimorum, tamen
omissis auctoritatibus ipsa re ac ratione exquirere pos-
10 sumus veritatem, atque hoc facilius, quod ea omnia,
quae a me adhuc dicta sunt, idem isti vera esse con-
cedunt, et necessarium bellum esse et magnum et in
uno Cn. Pompeio summa esse omnia.

*52–53. Hortensius says that the supreme command ought not to
be given to one man, but that objection has been answered by the
success of Pompey in his sole command against the pirates.*

52. Quid igitur ait Hortensius? Si uni omnia tribuenda sint, dignissimum esse Pompeium, sed ad unum
tamen omnia deferri non oportere. Obsolevit iam ista
oratio, re multo magis quam verbis refutata. Nam tu
5 idem, Q. Hortensi, multa pro tua summa copia ac
singulari facultate dicendi et in senatu contra virum
fortem, A. Gabinium, graviter ornateque dixisti, cum is
de uno imperatore contra praedones constituendo legem
promulgasset, et ex hoc ipso loco permulta item contra
10 eam legem verba fecisti. 53. Quid? tum, per deos immortales, si plus apud populum Romanum auctoritas
tua quam ipsius populi Romani salus et vera causa
valuisset, hodie hanc gloriam atque hoc orbis terrae
imperium teneremus? An tibi tum imperium hoc esse
15 videbatur, cum populi Romani legati, quaestores
praetoresque capiebantur? cum ex omnibus provinciis
commeatu et privato et publico prohibebamur? cum

ita clausa nobis erant maria omnia, ut neque privatam
rem transmarinam neque publicam iam obire possemus?

*54–55. Recently Rome has been so weak as to be unable to protect
even the ports and roads of Italy.*

XVIII. 54. Quae civitas antea umquam fuit—non
dico Atheniensium, quae satis late quondam mare
tenuisse dicitur, non Carthaginiensium, qui permultum
classe ac maritimis rebus valuerunt, non Rhodiorum,
quorum usque ad nostram memoriam disciplina navalis 5
et gloria permansit, quae civitas, inquam, antea tam
tenuis, aut tam parvola fuit, quae non portus suos et
agros et aliquam partem regionis atque orae maritimae
per se ipsa defenderet?   At hercule aliquot annos continuos ante legem Gabiniam ille populus Romanus, 10
cuius usque ad nostram memoriam nomen invictum in
navalibus pugnis permanserit, magna ac multo maxima
parte non modo utilitatis, sed dignitatis atque imperii
caruit.   55. Nos, quorum maiores Antiochum regem
classe Persemque superarunt omnibusque navalibus 15
pugnis Carthaginienses, homines in maritimis rebus
exercitatissimos paratissimosque, vicerunt, ii nullo in
loco iam praedonibus pares esse poteramus: nos, qui
antea non modo Italiam tutam habebamus, sed omnes
socios in ultimis oris auctoritate nostri imperii salvos 20
praestare poteramus, tum, cum insula Delos, tam procul a nobis in Aegaeo mari posita, quo omnes undique
cum mercibus atque oneribus commeabant, referta
divitiis, parva, sine muro, nihil timebat, idem non
modo provinciis atque oris Italiae maritimis ac portibus 25
nostris, sed etiam Appia iam via carebamus.   Et iis

temporibus non pudebat magistratus populi Romani
in hunc ipsum locum escendere, cum eum nobis maiores
nostri exuviis nauticis et classium spoliis ornatum
30 reliquissent.

> 56–58. *Pompey has, within one year, freed Rome from her
> humiliating position and yet is not allowed the privilege,
> granted to lesser men, of choosing his own* legatus. *If necessary,
> Cicero will himself raise the question of the appointment of
> Gabinius.*

XIX. 56. Bono te animo tum, Q. Hortensi, populus
Romanus et ceteros, qui erant in eadem sententia,
dicere existimavit ea quae sentiebatis, sed tamen in
salute communi idem populus Romanus dolori suo
5 maluit quam auctoritati vestrae obtemperare. Itaque
una lex, unus vir, unus annus non modo nos illa miseria
ac turpitudine liberavit, sed etiam effecit, ut aliquando
vere videremur omnibus gentibus ac nationibus terra
marique imperare. 57. Quo mihi etiam indignius
10 videtur obtrectatum esse adhuc, Gabinio dicam anne
Pompeio an utrique, id quod est verius, ne legaretur
A. Gabinius Cn. Pompeio expetenti ac postulanti.
Utrum ille, qui postulat ad tantum bellum legatum
quem velit, idoneus non est qui impetret, cum ceteri
15 ad expilandos socios diripiendasque provincias quos
voluerunt legatos eduxerint, an ipse, cuius lege salus
ac dignitas populo Romano atque omnibus gentibus
constituta est, expers esse debet gloriae eius imperatoris
atque eius exercitus, qui consilio ipsius ac periculo est
20 constitutus? 58. An C. Falcidius, Q. Metellus, Q.
Caelius Latiniensis, Cn. Lentulus, quos omnes honoris
causa nomino, cum tribuni pl. fuissent, anno proximo

legati esse potuerunt: in unc Gabinio sunt tam diligentes, qui in hoc bello, quod lege Gabinia geritur, in hoc imperatore atque exercitu, quem per vos ipse constituit, 25 etiam praecipuo iure esse deberet? De quo legando consules spero ad senatum relaturos: qui si dubitabunt aut gravabuntur, ego me profiteor relaturum, neque me impediet cuiusquam iniquitas, quo minus vobis fretus vestrum ius beneficiumque defendam, neque 30 praeter intercessionem quicquam audiam, de qua, ut arbitror, isti ipsi, qui minantur, etiam atque etiam quid liceat considerabunt. Mea quidem sententia, Quirites, unus A. Gabinius belli maritimi rerumque gestarum Cn. Pompeio socius ascribitur, propterea quod alter uni 35 illud bellum suscipiendum vestris suffragiis detulit, alter delatum susceptumque confecit.

59. The objection of Catulus, that if anything happened to Pompey there would be no one to take his place, has been answered by the people naming Catulus himself.

XX. 59. Reliquum est ut de Q. Catuli auctoritate et sententia dicendum esse videatur. Qui cum ex vobis quaereret, si in uno Cn. Pompeio omnia poneretis, si quid eo factum esset, in quo spem essetis habituri, cepit magnum suae virtutis fructum ac dignitatis, cum 5 omnes una prope voce in eo ipso vos spem habituros esse dixistis. Etenim talis est vir, ut nulla res tanta sit ac tam difficilis, quam ille non et consilio regere et integritate tueri et virtute conficere possit. Sed in hoc ipso ab eo vehementissime dissentio, quod, quo minus certa 10 est hominum ac minus diuturna vita, hoc magis res publica, dum per deos immortales licet, frui debet summi viri vita atque virtute.

*60. The objection that this proposal is without precedent can be
answered by pointing to past refusals of Rome to require a
precedent for action in time of war. There have, however, been
many precedents for this proposal.*

60. At enim ' ne quid novi fiat contra exempla atque
instituta maiorum.' Non dicam hoc loco, maiores
nostros semper in pace consuetudini, in bello utilitati
paruisse, semper ad novos casus temporum novorum
5 consiliorum rationes accommodasse; non dicam, duo
bella maxima, Punicum atque Hispaniense, ab uno
imperatore esse confecta duasque urbes potentissimas,
quae huic imperio maxime minitabantur, Carthaginem
atque Numantiam, ab eodem Scipione esse deletas; non
10 commemorabo, nuper ita vobis patribusque vestris esse
visum, ut in uno C. Mario spes imperii poneretur, ut
idem cum Iugurtha, idem cum Cimbris, idem cum
Teutonis bellum administraret: in ipso Cn. Pompeio, in
quo novi constitui nihil vult Q. Catulus, quam multa
15 sint nova summa Q. Catuli voluntate constituta recordamini.

*61–63. Throughout the whole of Pompey's career precedent
has been contravened with the approval of Catulus.*

XXI. 61. Quid tam novum quam adulescentulum
privatum exercitum difficili rei publicae tempore conficere? confecit; huic praeesse? praefuit; rem optime
ductu suo gerere? gessit. Quid tam praeter consue-
5 tudinem quam homini peradulescenti, cuius aetas a
senatorio gradu longe abesset, imperium atque exercitum dari, Siciliam permitti atque Africam bellumque
in ea provincia administrandum? Fuit in his provinciis singulari innocentia, gravitate, virtute; bellum

in Africa maximum confecit, victorem exercitum de- 10
portavit. Quid vero tam inauditum quam equitem
Romanum triumphare? at eam quoque rem populus
Romanus non modo vidit, sed omnium etiam studio
visendam et concelebrandam putavit. 62. Quid tam
inusitatum quam ut, cum duo consules clarissimi fortis- 15
simique essent, eques Romanus ad bellum maximum
formidolosissimumque pro consule mitteretur? missus
est. Quo quidem tempore cum esset non nemo in
senatu qui diceret ' non oportere mitti hominem privatum pro consule,' L. Philippus dixisse dicitur ' non se 20
illum sua sententia pro consule, sed pro consulibus
mittere.' Tanta in eo rei publicae bene gerendae spes
constituebatur, ut duorum consulum munus unius
adulescentis virtuti committeretur. Quid tam singu-
lare, quam ut ex senatus consulto legibus solutus consul 25
ante fieret, quam ullum alium magistratum per leges
capere licuisset? quid tam incredibile, quam ut iterum
eques Romanus ex senatus consulto triumpharet?
Quae in omnibus hominibus nova post hominum memoriam constituta sunt, ea tam multa non sunt quam 30
haec, quae in hoc uno homine vidimus. 63. Atque haec
tot exempla, tanta ac tam nova, profecta sunt in
eundem hominem a Q. Catuli atque a ceterorum
eiusdem dignitatis amplissimorum hominum auctoritate.   35

63–64. *It is intolerable that the will of the people should now be
opposed by the Senate whose proposals concerning Pompey
the people have always supported.*

XXII. Quare videant, ne sit periniquum et non
ferendum, illorum auctoritatem de Cn. Pompei digni-

tate a vobis comprobatam semper esse, vestrum ab illis
de eodem homine iudicium populique Romani auctori-
5 tatem improbari, praesertim cum iam suo iure populus
Romanus in hoc homine suam auctoritatem vel contra
omnes qui dissentiunt possit defendere, propterea quod
isdem istis reclamantibus vos unum illum ex omnibus
delegistis, quem bello praedonum praeponeretis. 64.
10 Hoc si vos temere fecistis et rei publicae parum consuluistis, recte isti studia vestra suis consiliis regere
conantur: sin autem vos plus tum in re publica vidistis,
vos istis repugnantibus per vosmet ipsos dignitatem
huic imperio, salutem orbi terrarum attulistis, aliquando
15 isti principes et sibi et ceteris populi Romani universi
auctoritati parendum esse fateantur.

64–68. *Not only are the military talents of Pompey required,
but also his moral integrity which will make him a leader
acceptable to the allies who have suffered so much from the avarice
of Rome's generals.*

Atque in hoc bello Asiatico et regio non solum
militaris illa virtus, quae est in Cn. Pompeio singularis,
sed aliae quoque virtutes animi magnae et multae
requiruntur. Difficile est in Asia, Cilicia, Syria
5 regnisque interiorum nationum ita versari nostrum
imperatorem, ut nihil aliud nisi de hoste ac de laude
cogitet. Deinde etiam si qui sunt pudore ac temperantia moderatiores, tamen eos esse tales propter multitudinem cupidorum hominum nemo arbitratur. 65.
10 Difficile est dictu, Quirites, quanto in odio simus apud
exteras nationes propter eorum, quos ad eas per hos
annos cum imperio misimus, libidines et iniurias. Quod
enim fanum putatis in illis terris nostris magistratibus

religiosum, quam civitatem sanctam, quam domum
satis clausam ac munitam fuisse? Urbes iam locupletes 15
et copiosae requiruntur, quibus causa belli propter
diripiendi cupiditatem inferatur. 66. Libenter haec
coram cum Q. Catulo et Q. Hortensio, summis et claris-
simis viris, disputarem; noverunt enim sociorum vul-
nera, vident eorum calamitates, querimonias audiunt. 20
Pro sociis vos contra hostes exercitum mittere putatis,
an hostium simulatione contra socios atque amicos?
Quae civitas est in Asia, quae non modo imperatoris aut
legati, sed unius tribuni militum animos ac spiritus
capere possit? XXIII. Quare etiam si quem habetis, 25
qui collatis signis exercitus regios superare posse
videatur, tamen, nisi erit idem, qui se a pecuniis
sociorum, qui ab eorum coniugibus ac liberis, qui ab
ornamentis fanorum atque oppidorum, qui ab auro
gazaque regia manus, oculos, animum cohibere possit, 30
non erit idoneus qui ad bellum Asiaticum regiumque
mittatur. 67. Ecquam putatis civitatem pacatam
fuisse, quae locuples sit? ecquam esse locupletem, quae
istis pacata esse videatur? Ora maritima, Quirites, Cn.
Pompeium non solum propter rei militaris gloriam, sed 35
etiam propter animi continentiam requisivit. Videbat
enim praetores locupletari quotannis pecunia publica
praeter paucos, neque nos quicquam aliud adsequi
classium nomine, nisi ut detrimentis accipiendis maiore
adfici turpitudine videremur. Nunc qua cupiditate 40
homines in provincias et quibus iacturis, quibus condicionibus proficiscantur, ignorant videlicet isti, qui ad
unum deferenda omnia esse non arbitrantur: quasi
vero Cn. Pompeium non cum suis virtutibus, tum etiam
alienis vitiis magnum esse videamus. 68. Quare nolite 45

dubitare quin huic uni credatis omnia, qui inter tot
annos unus inventus sit, quem socii in urbes suas cum
exercitu venisse gaudeant.

68. *This appointment is supported in Rome by men whose
authority is as great as that of its opponents.*

Quodsi auctoritatibus hanc causam, Quirites, con-
firmandam putatis, est vobis auctor vir bellorum
omnium maximarumque rerum peritissimus, P. Servilius, cuius tantae res gestae terra marique exstiterunt,
5 ut, cum de bello deliberetis, auctor vobis gravior nemo
esse debeat; est C. Curio, summis vestris beneficiis
adfectus maximisque rebus gestis, summo ingenio et
prudentia praeditus; est Cn. Lentulus, in quo omnes
pro amplissimis vestris honoribus summum consilium,
10 summam gravitatem esse cognovistis; est C. Cassius,
integritate, virtute, constantia singulari. Quare videte,
horumne auctoritatibus illorum orationi, qui dissentiunt, respondere posse videamur.

69–71. *An appeal to Manilius to persevere with his proposal;
a promise of all possible support for it; the speaker has nothing
to gain from giving his support; it is only given from a sense of
duty.*

XXIV. 69. Quae cum ita sint, C. Manili, primum
istam tuam et legem et voluntatem et sententiam laudo
vehementissimeque comprobo; deinde te hortor ut
auctore populo Romano maneas in sententia neve
5 cuiusquam vim aut minas pertimescas. Primum in te
satis esse animi perseverantiaeque arbitror; deinde
cum tantam multitudinem cum tanto studio adesse
videamus, quantam iterum nunc in eodem homine

praeficiendo videmus, quid est quod aut de re aut de
perficiendi facultate dubitemus? Ego autem, quic- 10
quid est in me studii, consilii, laboris, ingenii, quicquid
hoc beneficio populi Romani atque hac potestate
praetoria, quicquid auctoritate, fide, constantia possum,
id omne ad hanc rem conficiendam tibi et populo
Romano polliceor ac defero; 70. testorque omnes deos 15
et eos maxime, qui huic loco temploque praesident, qui
omnium mentes eorum, qui ad rem publicam adeunt,
maxime perspiciunt, me hoc neque rogatu facere cuiusquam, neque quo Cn. Pompei gratiam mihi per hanc
causam conciliari putem, neque quo mihi ex cuiusquam 20
amplitudine aut praesidia periculis aut adiumenta
honoribus quaeram, propterea quod pericula facile, ut
hominem praestare oportet, innocentia tecti repellemus,
honorem autem neque ab uno neque ex hoc loco, sed
eadem illa nostra laboriosissima ratione vitae, si vestra 25
voluntas feret, consequemur. 71. Quam ob rem, quicquid in hac causa mihi susceptum est, Quirites, id ego
omne me rei publicae causa suscepisse confirmo, tan-
tumque abest ut aliquam mihi bonam gratiam quaesisse
videar, ut multas me etiam simultates partim obscuras, 30
partim apertas intellegam, mihi non necessarias, vobis
non inutiles suscepisse. Sed ego me hoc honore prae-
ditum, tantis vestris beneficiis adfectum statui, Quirites,
vestram voluntatem et rei publicae dignitatem et
salutem provinciarum atque sociorum meis omnibus 35
commodis et rationibus praeferre oportere.

NOTES

Sections 1–3

I. 1. line 1. **mihi semper:** To be taken with **est visus** at the end of the concessive clause.

l. 1. **frequens conspectus vester:** ' the sight I have of your crowds ' **conspectus** is here passive in meaning. **frequens** when applied to the Senate sometimes has a technical meaning: that the number of senators required for the transaction of certain types of business is present, but here, as more usually, ' crowded '.

l. 2. **autem:** ' and '. There is no adversative force here.

l. 2. **locus:** The rostra in the Forum from which the people were addressed. It was so named after the *rostra* or ships' beaks adorning it, which had been taken from the captured vessels of the pirate town of Antium (the modern Anzio) in 338.

l. 2. **ad agendum ... ornatissimus: agendum** implies the phrase *cum populo*. This is the technical term for a magistrate laying a matter before the people in his official capacity. Only the senior magistrates had this right. **dicendum** is used of other speakers permitted by the presiding magistrate to address the people. **amplissimus** because of the distinction implied by the rank of such speakers, and **ornatissimus** because of the honour conferred in being permitted to speak.

l. 4. **tamen:** Introduces the main clause.

l. 4. **hoc aditu laudis:** An ablative of separation to be taken with **prohibuerunt. laudis** is an objective genitive ' have held me back from this road to fame '.

l. 4. **optimo cuique:** The common idiomatic use of a superlative adjective with **quisque** means ' all the most ... '. In this particular phrase **optimus** has a special meaning for Cicero; it covers all sound men who were likely to stand by the Republic in times of internal crisis. *pro Sest.* 97 lists the classes to be included in their number. Its meaning is not unlike what is now implied by the term ' the Establishment '.

l. 6. **vitae meae rationes**: ' my plan of life ', i.e. as a lawyer. The chief entry to political power for young men in Rome during this period lay through the law courts, particularly as counsel for the defence. By undertaking to defend fellow citizens the aspiring statesman sought to build up a following which would look to him as its patron and in recognition of his services give him political support.

l. 6. **ab ineunte aetate**: ' from my coming of age '. He was 26 years old when he delivered his first speech, *pro Quinctio* in 81.

l. 7. **antea per aetatem**: i.e. he did not take the opportunity of being invited by a magistrate to address the people, but preferred to wait until he could do so by right of his own office.

l. 8. **huius auctoritatem loci**: For once the English idiom is more concretely expressed than the Latin ' this place of influence '. auctoritatem is a favourite word of Cicero and is most frequently applied by him to the Senate. Indicating power based on prestige rather than on constitutional position, it is derived from *auctor* (cf. *auctoritatibus . . . auctor*, 68, p. 32.) and depicts prestige in action.

l. 9. **perfectum ingenio, elaboratum industria**: ' perfected by my mature talents and worked out by my application '.

l. 10. **amicorum temporibus transmittendum**: ' ought to be made over to my friends in their time of peril '. tempus and temporibus are used in different senses. This double use of the same word in close proximity was a recognized device of ancient oratory. See Introduction, p. xviii.

2. **line 11. Ita**: Goes with the second main verb. Make the first clause subordinate in English. Cicero has made these clauses co-ordinate for the rhetorical effect of the contrast.

l. 12. **vacuus . . . ab**: ' without '.

l. 12. **vestram causam**: ' your interests ', but the audience is being addressed as Roman citizens (Quirites), and therefore this =' the interests of the state '.

l. 12. **defenderent**: A consecutive subjunctive; ' those fit to champion your interests ' not ' those who championed . . .'.

l. 13. **caste integreque**: i.e. without breaking the laws

forbidding a lawyer to be paid or those aimed at preventing collusion (*praevaricatio*).

l. 14. **iudicio:** In electing Cicero praetor.

l. 15. **dilationem:** Elections could be stopped by the *obnuntiatio* of a magistrate or augur reporting unpropitious omens, by the *intercessio* of a tribune interposing his veto, or — increasingly in this century — by mob violence. We know that violence attended the passage of the *lex Gabinia* (see Introduction, p. xxxix) and the *lex Roscia*, which redistributed the allocation of seats in the theatre in the year of Cicero's election; and this is the most likely cause.

l. 16. **comitiorum ... renuntiatus sum:** Magistrates *cum imperio* (i.e. praetors and consuls of the annual magistrates) were elected by the *comitia centuriata*, traditionally instituted by the king, Servius Tullius, but probably not dating further back than 450. These *comitia* were never fully democratic because the voting groups were unequal and the wealthier citizens had a controlling influence.

The procedure was as follows: The site of the elections was divided into as many *saepta* (enclosures) as there were centuries. Voting then took place in secret under the provision of various *leges tabellariae* passed in the second half of the second century, and the votes were recorded on the official tablets (*tabellae*) from which the laws got their name. A *centuria praerogativa* was chosen by lot from the seventy *centuriae* of the first of the five classes and had the right to vote first. The votes were counted by centuries and a majority of votes in each century decided its vote, a majority of the centuries deciding the will of the *comitia*. The voting of the *centuria praerogativa* set the pattern of subsequent voting which all took place simultaneously.

What appears to have happened in Cicero's case is that on two occasions the elections got far enough for his election to have been completed and the announcement made, but only at the third attempt was the business validly finished.

l. 16. **primus:** First among the eight praetors to be elected.

l. 17. **quid ... praescriberetis:** i.e. that they should do as Cicero had done.

l. 19. **auctoritatis:** Partitive genitive with **tantum:** 'influence' as a result of the unanimous election to high office.

l. 19. **honoribus mandandis:** 'by entrusting me with office '.

l. 20. **ad agendum:** sc. *cum populo.*

l. 21. **forensi usu:** 'experience in court '. The law courts sat in the Forum or in the *basilicae* surrounding it.

l. 23. **apud eos:** 'before those men '.

l. 25. **possum:** 'I have the ability ', not 'if I *shall* be able ' which would require the future.

l. 25. **qui ... duxerunt:** 'whose verdict has asserted that oratory too deserved reward ', lit. 'who thought in their judgement that to that thing [ability in speaking] too a reward ought to be given '.

3. l. 26. **Atque:** Introduces a further point. The Latin order must be altered to obtain idiomatic English. The **illud** looks forward to what follows and the main verb comes after the clause it introduces.

l. 28. **in hac ... dicendi:** Take this phrase together. **insolita** because it was his first speech **ex hoc loco** (the rostra), i.e. political.

l. 29. **oratio:** Here 'language' as opposed to **orationis** below 'subject-matter '. Cf. the use of the word in 52, p. 24.

l. 29. **possit:** Another consecutive subjunctive.

l. 31. **virtute:** The qualities needed for high command.

l. 31. **difficilius ... quaerendus est:** A piece of conventional flattery. Cicero does not have to search for material for his subject, but so abundant is it he has to limit it.

Sections 4–5

II. 4. line 1. **inde:** Another forward-looking word placed early in the sentence.

l. 2. **ducitur:** 'begins '.

l. 2. **bellum:** See Introduction, pp. xxviii f.

l. 3. **vectigalibus:** From the adjective **vectigalis,** here used as a masculine noun: 'tributaries '.

l. 3. **sociis:** While Rome was still only an Italian power her alliances were made within Italy with *socii* who were bound to contribute to the common army when called upon to do so, and who appreciated Rome's predominant status in the alliance. When, however, at the beginning of the second century Rome joined, as an equal, coalitions with states beyond the boundaries of Italy — particularly in Greece and the East — the phrase *socii et amici* was found to cover this new relationship. These *amici* were not at first under any obligation to aid Rome, but neutrality came to be frowned upon, and Rome did not hesitate in times of war to exert pressure upon states to join actively in the common effort and do her will. The Italian *socius* and the Greek *amicus* were originally quite different, but, as Rome's power grew, the distinction became blurred and the status of these Greek and Eastern allies was soon reduced to one similar to that of the earlier *socii*. The term *socii* came to be applied freely to provincials, although with a very changed meaning from the original, and the kings of regions on provincial borders were recognized as *socii et amici*. The position of these kings was ambiguous, and the term ' client ' kings gives a better idea of the Roman view of their relationship with her. Rome tended to treat them as a *patronus* treated his *clientes*.

l. 4. **Mithridate:** See Introduction, pp. xxi f.

l. 4. **Tigrane:** Tigranes I ' the Great ' became king of Armenia in the first decade of the century. He allied himself with Mithridates and carved a short-lived empire for himself out of the north of Parthia, with its capital at Tigranocerta. He lost his capital to Lucullus, but was not finally subdued until Pompey separated him from Mithridates. Only Armenia proper was left under his control, and thereafter he remained at peace with Rome. See Introduction, pp. xxiii f.

l. 5. **relictus:** ' left alone ', i.e. after he had sought refuge with Tigranes in 72.

l. 5. **lacessitus:** By Lucullus's invasion of Armenia in 69.

l. 5. **occupandam:** ' seize ', ' lay hold of '. Only ' occupy ' in the purely military sense.

l. 6. **Asiam:** The Roman province of Asia, at this time consisting of Phrygia, Mysia, Caria, and Lydia. See frontispiece map, pp. viii and ix.

l. 6. **arbitrantur:** As if Cicero had written **qui,** not **quorum.**

l. 6. **Equitibus Romanis:** A clear account of the taxation systems in operation in the provinces at this time is to be found in J. R. Hawthorn, *The Republican Empire,* pp. 41 f. The collection of taxes had come to be under the control of wealthy and influential *equites* in the following way. The Romans dissolved the native governments which had previously ruled the provinces but had no Civil Service to put in their place. As a result the collection of taxes was made the responsibility either of the individual *civitas* which paid them to the Roman governor direct or of a private firm employed by the Romans to do the job for them.

The second method was that employed in Asia with the important difference that now the taxes for the whole province, not for each state individually, were auctioned in Rome. By the end of the second century the capital required to bid successfully at these auctions had become so great that only the wealthiest companies could raise it and, since senators were forbidden by the *lex Claudia* of 218 to take part in business, large equestrian *societates* were formed to undertake the task of tax-collection for the state.

As Cicero fairly points out in this passage the capital outlay and risk to capital were considerable but, even allowing for these factors, the profits sought by these companies were enormous. See also 17–19, pp. 8–9.

l. 7. **honestissimis viris:** 'distinguished gentlemen'. A regular epithet for the knights. **honestus** does not mean ' honest '.

l. 8. **magnae res aguntur:** ' large sums of money are at stake ', i.e. the capital expended upon obtaining the right to farm the province's taxes and financing the organization of collection.

l. 9. **pro necessitudine:** ' in view of my close ties '. Cicero was connected by birth with the Equestrian Order (See Introduction, p. xi) and in the 70s his activity in the Courts was often on behalf of the equestrian *publicani*. Since the *Equites,* and their financial interests in particular, were the main force behind the proposals of the *lex Gabinia* and *lex Manilia,* his *necessitudo* will have provided a powerful motive for him to

speak in support of this bill. In this passage and in 17–19
pp. 8–9, he would win the goodwill of the *Equites* which he
extended this year by undertaking the defence of Cluentius, a
member of the Equestrian Order with many powerful friends.

l. 10. **ordine:** At this time there were three principal classes:
the *ordines senatorius, equester* and *plebeius.* Here the *ordo
equester*, but *ordo* by itself when the context does not clearly
indicate otherwise regularly refers to the Senate.

l. 11. **detulerunt:** ' have reported '.

5. line 11. **Bithyniae:** In north-west Asia Minor. See
frontispiece map. Nicomedes IV, the last king, was driven
from his kingdom by Mithridates but was restored to his throne
in 92. His raids into Pontus started the First Mithridatic War
in 88, and he was again restored by Rome in 84, and then ruled
until his death ten years later, when he bequeathed his kingdom
to Rome. See Introduction, pp. xxiii f.

l. 12. **exustos esse:** *ex-* is an intensifying prefix ' burnt to the
ground '. This and the following infinitives show that we are
being given the contents of the letters of the knights, and the
passage is therefore in indirect speech.

l. 13. **Ariobarzanis:** King of Cappadocia. See frontispiece
map. He had been repeatedly driven from his kingdom by
Mithridates and restored by Rome. He seems to have been in
possession of it from the Treaty of Dardanus in 85 until 66 when
Tigranes attacked him. See Introduction, pp. xxiii f.

l. 14. **vectigalibus:** ' tributary states '.

l. 14. **L. Lucullum:** The consul of 74, he had been given an
extraordinary command for the war against Mithridates and
had left for the East. He invaded Pontus and forced Mithridates
to flee to Tigranes in 71. Two years later he invaded Armenia
and defeated Tigranes. See also Introduction, pp. xxix f., and
note on 10, **initia . . . videantur,** p. 45.

l. 16. **huic cui successerit:** M'. Acilius Glabrio, the consul of
67, who found in Asia not the easy triumph for which he had
hurried off, but a discontented army and much hard fighting.
As a result he refused to move from Bithynia. **successerit** is
subjunctive because it is the verb of a subordinate clause in

indirect speech. The subjunctive mood is used in this type of clause because the clause is part of a statement for which the speaker disclaims responsibility. The indicatives of the other relative clauses in this chapter show that they are comments inserted by Cicero, and not part of what the knights wrote.

l. 18. **deposci atque expeti:** ' is demanded with all possible vigour '. English often prefers to intensify a verb by adding an adverb or adverbial phrase, whereas Latin increases the emphasis by adding another verb of similar meaning.

Section 6

6. line 1. **Causa:** ' situation ', ' nature of the case '. Watch order in translating.

l. 2. **genere . . . magnitudine:** i.e. it is the sort of war that we must fight and its importance needs measures adequate for so large a conflict.

l. 6. **persequendi studium:** ' a desire to see it through to the end '.

l. 6. **debeat:** Consecutive subjunctive.

l. 6. **agitur:** ' is involved '.

l. 7. **cum . . . tum:** ' great indeed in . . ., but greatest of all in . . .'. This pair of words is regularly used to express climax.

l. 9. **sociorum atque amicorum:** See note on sociis, p. 37.

l. 11. **certissima . . . maxima:** Even Cicero, by the standards of his time a humane and progressive man in his attitude towards provincials and one prepared to fight cruelty and corruption in provincial governors, sees the matter as one of Roman prestige and the province itself primarily as a source of revenue.

l. 12. **ornamenta:** The outward signs of the rise in standards of living that the wealth from Asia would bring to Rome in times of peace.

l. 13. **bona:** The investments of the knights and the possessions of the Italian trading community.

l. 13. **a vobis:** **a** with the ablative of the agent instead of the dative to avoid confusion with **quibus,** dative with **est consulendum.**   Remember *te consulo* = I consult you, *tibi consulo* = I consult your interests.

Sections 7–8

III. 7. line 1. **appetentes:** The participial adjective is regularly followed by an objective genitive. Cf. 51, **rei publicae**, p. 23.

l. 3. **macula:** ' blot ', ' stain '.

l. 3. **Mithridatico bello superiore:** i.e. the First Mithridatic War, not counting the less important campaign fought by Murena. See Introduction, p. xxiii.

l. 5. **quod:** ' in that '.

l. 5. **uno die:** In 88. As a deliberate act of policy, to show to the provincials that Roman authority was ended, he ordered a simultaneous massacre throughout the province of all Romans and Italians. 80,000 are said to have been slaughtered.

l. 6. **civitatibus:** The Greek cities of Asia Minor.

l. 8. **denotavit:** ' marked down '. This use of the gerundive predicatively in agreement with the direct object of a verb is found in earlier Latin, but was greatly extended by Cicero and subsequent authors. Cf. the English: ' He had them killed '.

l. 10. **ita . . . ut:** Consecutive clauses in which the pattern of the sentence is **regnat, et ita regnat ut . . .** or **triumphavit, sed ita triumphaverunt ut . . .** (8 below, p. 4) are used to limit the first statement, and are common in Cicero. Rephrasing of the sentence is necessary in translation ' but he ruled for a further twenty-two years, a king unwilling to skulk in the fastnesses of Pontus or even of Cappadocia, but sallying forth . . .'.

l. 11. **emergere . . . versari:** sc. **velit.** For the historical background, see Introduction, pp. xxiii f.

l. 12. **patrio:** ' hereditary ', i.e. Pontus. He had added Cappadocia to his domains in the last decade of the previous century.

l. 12. **vectigalibus:** Masculine again, almost certainly. It could, however, mean ' in the midst of your revenues ', but this is unlikely.

8. line 15. **insignia victoriae:** i.e. triumphs — but not the final victory.

l. 16. **L. Sulla:** L. Cornelius Sulla, the victor over Mithridates in the First Mithridatic War and subsequently dictator. Owing to the civil war following his return to Italy from the East, he did not celebrate his triumph until 81.

l. 16. **L. Murena:** L. Licinius Murena was left by Sulla in 84 as propraetor in Asia where he deliberately provoked the Second Mithridatic War by his aggression. He was defeated by Mithridates and after being ordered by Sulla to cease fighting returned to Rome in 81. Later in the same year he celebrated an ill-deserved triumph, ambition for which had made him start the war. See Introduction, pp. xxvii f.

l. 19. **Verum tamen:** ' But nevertheless '.

l. 20. **quod egerunt ... quod reliquerunt:** Either ' for what they did ... for what they left undone ' taking **quod** as the direct object of the verbs and understanding the antecedent, or alternatively, as is preferable, take **quod** as a conjunction and the two verbs absolutely. The use of **ago** in this way is well attested, and it would be easy to extend the use to the parallel verb **relinquo.** In this case, translate: ' we must praise them for being active and forgive them for leaving their work unfinished'.

l. 21. **res publica:** ' the condition of the state'. While Sulla was in the East the Marians had re-established themselves in Rome, and the rapidity with which he organised Asia and the mildness of the terms imposed upon Mithridates, show Sulla's eagerness to return to Italy and regain his political authority.

Sections 9-11

IV. 9. line 1. **reliquum:**   i.e.   that   followed   Murena's departure.

l. 2. **oblivionem ... comparationem:** Variety is obtained by the use of two abstract nouns derived from verbs rather than the gerund or gerundive. The meaning is the same: ' to blot out the memory of the old war ...'.

l. 3. **contulit:** *aliquid ad aliquid conferre* = to devote something to some purpose.

l. 3. **ornassetque:** ' and had equipped '.

l. 5. **potuisset**: We should expect **posset** but the proximity of the pluperfect subjunctives may well have attracted this verb into their tense, although the time of its action is simultaneous with **comparasset**.

l. 5. **Bosporanis**: After the end of the First Mithridatic War, Mithridates had to suppress revolts in Colchis and the Cimmerian Bosporus (the modern Crimea). See map pp. viii and ix. His operations were interrupted by Murena's raids, but even after Murena's recall he was unable successfully to complete them.

simularet: 'he pretended' (that he was doing something that he was not). The opposite is **dissimulare**. His pretence lay in making out that this war — real enough — was the cause of all his preparations.

l. 6. **Hispaniam**: This was one of the alliances by means of which Mithridates hoped to hold off Rome.

l. 7. **duces**: Rhetorical plural: only Sertorius is meant. See Introduction, p. xviii. Sertorius had been sent in 83 to govern Nearer Spain and had proceeded to organize it as a Marian bastion against Sulla. Roman generals sent to recover the province were defeated by his Romano-Iberian power, and in 77 Pompey was dispatched against him by the Senate. He, too, met with little success, and it was probably in the winter of 76–75 that the negotiations between Mithridates and Sertorius were conducted. Mithridates offered ships and money in return for recognition of his claims to Asia Minor. Sertorius, however, was only willing to recognize the claims to Bithynia and Cappadocia and to supply a military mission to teach Roman methods of warfare.

l. 9. **disiunctissimis** ... **diversis**: 'very far apart ... very different'.

l. 9. **binis**: The distributive numeral is used with the plural of nouns whose numbers have different meanings: **copia** = plenty, abundance; **copiae** = troops, forces.

l. 11. **ancipiti contentione districti**: 'engaged in a struggle on two fronts'. **ancipiti** here with its root meaning. Mithridates's excellent strategy never came to anything owing to the collapse of the war in Spain after the murder of Sertorius in 72.

l. 11. **de imperio:** 'for world dominion'.

10. line 12. **alterius partis:** 'on the western front'.

l. 13. **plus firmamenti ac roboris:** 'more support and a more vigorous backing'.

l. 14. **divino:** 'inspired'. This passage gives an inflated estimate of Pompey's individual contribution to success. The war-weariness of the Spanish tribes and the death of their leader were more telling factors than any strategy or leadership of Pompey's.

l. 15. **res:** 'the campaign'.

l. 16. **initia . . . videantur:** The strategic and tactical ability of Lucullus were first class, and it was upon them that his military successes rested. His subsequent failures were brought about by his deficiencies as a leader. He failed to hold the loyalty of his troops, and his salutary reorganization of Asiatic affairs, intended to alleviate the burden caused by Sulla's indemnity, earned him the bitter hatred of the Roman financiers. In 68 this had compelled the government to deprive him of the province of Asia, and in 67 his army's discipline collapsed and he was forced to remain inactive. It was he who broke Mithridates but he could not finish the war. See also Introduction, p. xxix f., for a more detailed account of his early successes and later failures.

l. 17. **non felicitati . . . sed fortunae:** Note the oratorical antithesis and chiasmic order. Chiasmus is the figure of speech named after the Greek letter *chi* from the way in which it was set out diagramatically: e.g.

felicitati   virtuti

χ

culpae   fortunae

For a well-known example of this figure of speech in English, cf. Luke xvi. 3: 'I cannot dig; to beg I am ashamed.'

It may be that today military historians pay too little attention to luck, but it is certain that in the ancient world luck was believed to play a far greater part in a general's successes or failures than is allowed to it today. Even making allowance, however, for this shift of emphasis, we should always be on our guard when we meet such rhetorical figures of speech, lest the writer is more interested in them than in an accurate analysis of the events.

l. 20. **alio loco:** See 20, p. 9.

l. 21. **ei:** With verbs of ' depriving ' Latin uses the dative of the person deprived, not, as we might expect, the ablative of separation. This use of the dative to denote the person to whose disadvantage the act is performed is to be explained by the fact that in Latin constructions tend to develop in pairs of opposites; and this particular use has grown up on the analogy of the dative of the indirect object after verbs of ' giving '. The ablative with a preposition is normal with a thing or place. ·

11. line 22. **de:** ' as to ', ' as for '.

l. 23. **exorsus:** The first part of the speech, not the introduction.

l. 24. **videte ... putetis: Videte** and **putetis** are not merely repetitive. Cicero's audience is being asked to consider the situation, not with a view to action but to forming an opinion about it: ' consider with what inspiration you should in your view be moved '.

Sections 11–13

V. line 1. **saepe ... gesserunt;** Piracy was endemic in the Mediterranean during the republican period and was only finally suppressed by Augustus. The beaks decorating the Rostra were from the pirate stronghold of Antium destroyed in 338, and wars were fought in 229 and 219 against the Adriatic pirates. In the second century both Rome and the Hellenistic states disbanded their navies, leaving an unpoliced Mediterranean in which piracy was rampant; it reached its height during the first century B.C. A succession of campaigns was fought during the forty years before Pompey appeared on the scene. In 102 the praetor, M. Antonius, conducted a campaign against the pirates off the south coast of Asia Minor and established the province of Cilicia; P. Servilius Vatia Isauricus, the proconsul of Cilicia from 78 to 74, made a systematic attempt to clear them from southern Asia Minor; M. Antonius Creticus, the son of the praetor of 102, was himself praetor in

74 and for two years waged an unsuccessful war against them; and in 68 to 66 Q. Caecilius Metellus Creticus conquered the pirate base of Crete.

l. 1. **mercatoribus . . . tractatis:** Ablative absolute with a causal connection with the finite verb. **mercatoribus . . . naviculariis,** 'traders . . . ship-owners'. **iniuriosius tractatis,** i.e. having suffered nothing nearly so bad as the fate of Romans at the hands of Mithridates.

l. 2. **vos:** Strongly contrasted with **Maiores nostri.** English would insert a conjunction.

l. 3. **tot . . . necatis:** See 7, p. 4.

l. 4. **tandem:** In questions means 'I ask you'. Cf. the famous beginning of Cat. I. *Quo usque tandem abutere, Catilina, patientia nostra?* and further examples below.

l. 5. **appellati superbius:** 'addressed rather disrespectfully'. In 146 the Roman envoys attending a meeting of the Achaean League were insulted and, according to some accounts, ill-treated. It suits Cicero's purpose to ignore the tradition of personal violence since he is concerned to contrast the mere insults repaid by war in the past with the recent slaughter which his contemporaries hesitate to revenge.

l. 6. **lumen:** Figurative 'glory'.

l. 6. **exstinctum esse:** Note the tense of the infinitive and that it agrees with **lumen,** not **Corinthum** (f.), owing to the close connection in sense between the predicate and the word in apposition.

l. 7. **vos:** See above.

l. 8. **legatum:** M'. Aquilius, consul in 101, was, as legate in 88, driven from Bithynia by Mithridates, captured, and killed by having molten gold poured down his throat; a fitting reply, it was held, to Roman avarice.

l. 10. **libertatem . . . imminutam:** 'any restriction upon the liberty of . . .'. Latin regularly uses a participle where a verbal noun would be more natural in English.

l. 12. **persecuti sunt:** 'avenged'.

l. 13. **relinquetis?:** sc. 'unavenged'.

12. line 13. **Videte:** Cicero's theme is a commonplace of ancient oratory and phrased in the direct contrast so beloved of classical orators. ne ' that not ' has the subjunctive **sit.** The correlative **ut** ' as ' is followed by the indicative.

l. 16. **tueri et conservare:** ' protect and keep safe '.

l. 17. **Quid?:** Introduces a new point.

l. 17. **quod:** ' the fact that '.

l. 18. **vocatur:** Often has this transferred meaning of placing in a certain position.

l. 19. **Ariobarzanes:** See Introduction, pp. xxiii f.

l. 19. **socius ... atque amicus:** See note on **sociis** above, p. 37.

l. 22. **cuncta Asia atque Graecia:** Ablative of place. The preposition — in this case it would be *in* — is often omitted when the noun is qualified by *summus, imus, medius, totus, omnis, cunctus,* or *universus.*

l. 23. **exspectare:** ' to await eagerly '.

l. 24. **imperatorem ... certum:** ' any particular general '.

l. 25. **cum praesertim:** Watch word-order.

l. 25. **alium:** i.e. not the general they wanted. This was M'. Acilius Glabrio, consul in 67.

l. 26. **periculo:** i.e. at the hands of Glabrio or Lucullus.

13. line 27. **sentiunt:** ' perceive '.

l. 27. **hoc idem quod vos:** Lit. ' this same thing which you see . . .'. Translate ' just as you yourselves do '.

l. 28. **in quo ... omnia:** ' whose qualifications are in every respect the highest '. For these qualifications see 36 and 51, pp. 17 and 51.

l. 29. **propter:** Here an adverb: ' in the area ', ' close at hand '. Cf. 16, p. 7, for another example. Pompey was in Cilicia where he had wintered after the end of his campaign against the pirates in 67 and 66.

l. 29. **aegrius:** They are all the sorrier that they are not having his help because he is so near them.

l. 30. **adventu ipso atque nomine:** ' by the mere fact of his arrival and by his reputation alone '.

l. 31. **venerit:** The perfect subjunctive in indirect statement after **intellegunt** represents the perfect indicative of direct speech.

l. 30. **maritimum bellum:** Against the pirates.

l. 31. **tamen:** Shows the beginning of the main sentence after a concessive clause and in this use is regularly first word.

l. 31. **repressos ... ac retardatos:** ' checked and delayed ', To attribute the decline in the power of Mithridates to the influence of Pompey does less than justice to Lucullus.

l. 33. **taciti:** Cicero apparently avoids the derivative adverb but in general Latin uses an adjective agreeing with the subject, rather than an adverb qualifying the verb, which is the normal English usage.

l. 33. **ut ... existimetis:** Indirect command.

l. 35. **commendetis:** Consecutive subjunctive as in *Dignus est qui puniatur* ' He is worthy of punishment '.

l. 35. **atque ...:** ' and this all the more, because '.

l. 37. **imperio:** The power held by the curule magistrates (i.e. consuls and praetors) who governed the provinces. The power of the lower magistrates was *potestas*.

l. 37. **ut ... differant:** For more upon provincial mis-government, see 65, p. 30. **adventus in urbes;** in English a prepositional phrase may be either adverbial or adjectival, in Latin it may only be adverbial and it therefore cannot normally qualify a noun. If, however, the noun was derived from a verb, no objection was felt to qualifying it with such a phrase. Here **adventus** is sufficiently close to the verb **advenio** for it to be qualified by **in urbes.**

l. 39. **hunc ... vident:** ' they previously heard and now see in front of them this man of such ... that ...'.

l. 40. **temperantia , ..:** These qualities portray an idealised Pompey. His standards of provincial government were certainly higher than those of many of his contemporaries, but his ' moderation ', ' gentleness ', and ' kindness ' are qualities which propaganda claimed for leaders such as Pompey, and which the picture of him painted by ancient writers does not confirm.

l. 43. **commoretur**: Subjunctive because it represents part of what the provincials say, and is therefore a subordinate clause in indirect speech.

Sections 14–16

VI. 14. line 1. **Quare, si ...**: Watch word-order in translating.

l. 1. **propter socios**: Genuine concern for her allies played a small part in Rome's considerations. Sometimes she seized upon a comparatively minor affray involving an ally and used it as a *casus belli*; at others she used her allies to bring about a situation in which she could justifiably start a war which she desired for her own ends. In all the cases cited by Cicero Rome's eyes were on her own advantage in a wider field than that suggested by the alleged cause for her declaration of war.

l. 1. **nulla ipsi iniuria lacessiti**: ' although not provoked by any injury to themselves '.

l. 2. **cum Antiocho**: The Romans fought Antiochus the Great in a war (192–188) to protect their allies among the Greeks of Asia Minor.

l. 2. **cum Philippo**: Philip V of Macedon upon whom the Romans declared war in 200 for assisting the Acarnanians' attack on Athens.

l. 3. **cum Aetolis**: They assisted Antiochus in his war against Rome.

l. 3. **cum Poenis**: The First Punic War was caused by the help Rome gave in 264 to the Mamertines, a body of mercenary troops, who had twenty-five years previously seized the Sicilian town of Messana; the Second by Hannibal's attack in 219 upon Saguntum, Rome's ally in Spain; and the Third by the attack upon Rome's ally Masinissa, king of Numidia, who goaded the Carthaginians into breaking their treaty with Rome.

l. 4. **convenit**: Impersonal.

l. 5. **dignitate**: The respect which you feel is due to anyone or anything. ' honour '.

l. 5. **praesertim cum**: Cicero, after all his fine talk about helping wronged allies and Rome's imperial honour, lets the cat out of the bag. Nor was his tongue in his cheek when he said this.

l. 6. **de . . . agatur?**: ' your most important revenues are at stake '. Cf. 6, p. 3, for the more usual usage **vectigalia aguntur.** We should expect **agitur de vectigalibus** to mean ' your taxes are under discussion '.

l. 7. **tanta sunt:** ' are so great and no more ', ' are scarcely adequate '. **tantus** expresses only relative size, and is therefore used with a following **ut** to denote a small amount, extent, etc.

l. 8. **iis . . . contenti esse:** ' to be satisfied with them '.

l. 10. **ubertate . . . fructuum:** The land upon which crops were grown and which produced revenue in the form of tithes, *decumae.* This tax was paid upon crops other than corn. See II *Verr.* iii. 16. *vini et olei decumas et frugum minutarum.*

l. 10. **magnitudine pastionis:** This produced the capitation tax levied for the right of pasturing cattle, *scriptura.*

l. 11. **multitudine . . . exportantur:** Exports produced customs dues, *portoria.* **exportantur** is indicative because **earum . . . exportantur** means no more than ' exports '. Use of the subjunctive would introduce consideration of what the exports were.

l. 13. **belli . . . dignitatem:** The orator's way of saying ' the revenues which enable you to wage war and raise your standard of living in time of peace '.

15. line 16. **venit:** Perfect indicative.

l. 18. **ipse:** ' mere '.

l. 20. **pecua:** ' pastures '. Normally an ante-classical word, but its use here is attested by Servius in his commentary on Virgil, written in the fourth century A.D.

l. 22. **portu:** ' harbour dues '.

l. 22. **scriptura:** So called from the written list in the records of the *publicani* stating the number of cattle pastured on the public land.

16. line 26. **pensitant:** Again indicative although the verb of a subordinate clause in indirect speech. **eos, qui . . . pensitant** means ' our taxpayers '.

l. 27. **exercent atque exigunt:** The first verb refers to those who control the collection of taxes, the *publicani*; the second to those who do the actual collecting. They might be *publicani* working in the province in person but would more often be employees, *familiae*, of the *societas* or company of *publicani*.

l. 30. **saltibus:** ' pastures '.

l. 31. **custodiis:** Stations to prevent the evasion of *portoria*.

l. 33. **fructui:** ' a source of revenue '. A predicative dative with the usual accompanying dative of the person interested.

l. 35. **liberatos?:** ' in a state of having been freed '. Cicero emphasizes by his choice of this participle rather than **liberos** the positive measures which Rome must take.

Sections 17-19

VII. 17. line 1. **Ac ne illud quidem ...:** This marks a new point. ' Nor should you overlook this fact either ...'. **vobis** is a dative of the agent with the gerundive **neglegendum.** This use of the case is also found with the perfect participle passive.

l. 2. **quod ... proposueram:** ' which I had intended to take last '.

l. 2. **cum essem ... dicturus:** ' when I started to speak '.

l. 4. **pertinet:** The subject is **belli genus** to be understood from the previous clause.

l. 4. **pro:** ' in accordance with '.

l. 5. **habenda est ratio:** *rationem habere* =' to take account of '.

l. 5. **et:** ' firstly '.

l. 6. **honestissimi atque ornatissimi:** ' of good standing and well-to-do ' (lit. ' well-equipped ').

l. 7. **rationes et copias:** ' their business and resources '. Cicero's argument is that the *publicani* have invested their money in the task of collecting Rome's provincial taxes for her and are therefore entitled to expect her protection.

l. 8. **ipsorum per se:** i.e. without consideration of others.

l. 9. **nervos:** ' sinews '. Both Latin and English use the anatomical metaphor.

l. 10. **duximus:** ' have thought '.

l. 10. **exercet:** ' farm '. See note on 16, p. 52.

l. 11. **firmamentum:** ' prop ', ' pillar ', ' support '. The metaphor has changed.

l. 11. **ceterorum ordinum:** i.e. all members of the state other than the *publicani*.

18. line 12. **Deinde:** ' Secondly '.

l. 12. **ex ceteris ordinibus:** Either ' from the other classes ' taking **ordinibus** to have the same meaning as **ordinum** in 17 above, or ' from the other companies ' taking it in a narrower sense to refer to the merchants, shipowners and others who were in the same broad class as the *publicani*. The distinction should not be pressed. The first part of the sentence makes better sense if **ordinibus** is taken in the second way, yet **partim ipsi . . . debetis** must refer to the senators, who were forbidden by a *lex Claudia* of 218 to take part in large-scale commerce, but who often had money invested in companies of *publicani*, and held land abroad.

l. 13. **partim ipsi . . . partim eorum:** in the first case **partim** is an adverb; in the second, a noun with a partitive genitive depending upon it. Cicero could have as well written **alii . . . alii.**

l. 15. **pecunias magnas collocatas habent:** ' have large sums of money invested '. Beware of translating as if Cicero had written *pecunias multas collocaverunt.*

l. 16. **humanitatis vestrae. . . sapientiae:** Possessive genitives ' it is the mark of '.

l. 18. **a re publica:** Compressed for **a rei publicae calamitate.**

l. 19. **illud parvi refert:** ' it is of little importance '. **illud** refers to the rest of the sentence. **parvi** is a genitive of price, one of the adverbial uses of the case.

l. 19. **nos . . . recuperare:** ' that we can by a later victory win back the revenues lost by the tax-farmers '. **publicanis** is in this translation taken as a dative of the agent, but it could be ' win back for the tax-farmers the revenues they have lost '. The argument is that there would be nobody to collect the taxes, which would therefore be useless to Rome. The existing *publicani* would have lost their capital, and new men would not take on so risky a venture.

l. 21. **redimendi**: ' of hiring ', ' of farming '.

19. line 23. **quod**: The accusative of the relative pronoun of which **id,** itself the object of **retinere,** is the antecedent. Note that **doceo** takes two accusatives; the more common construction in classical Latin is an accusative and infinitive.

l. 23. **eadem Asia**: ' that same Asia '.

l. 24. **initio**: Temporal ablative; ' at the beginning '.

l. 24. **belli Asiatici**: The Third Mithridatic War.

l. 24. **docuit**: Singular, although there are two connected subjects. It is easy to understand how Asia and Mithridates could very easily be felt to represent a single idea.

l. 24. **quidem**: Emphasizes **id.** We should probably obtain the same effect by tone of voice.

l. 26. **tum**: To be taken with **concidisse.**

l. 26. **amiserant**: When a *cum*-clause indicates the time at which the action of the main clause takes place, i.e. dates it, the indicative is always used. **amisisset** here would mean that the collapse of credit at Rome occurred after the losses in Asia.

l. 27. **solutione ... concidisse**: ' credit collapsed owing to non-payment of debts '.

l. 29. **ut non**: Introduces a negative consecutive clause. Lit. ' so as not to '. Translate by ' without ' and verbal noun.

l. 30. **A quo periculo**: Latin commonly puts first in a sentence any reference to the subject-matter of the previous sentence, particularly if emphasis is required.

l. 31. **haec fides ... pecuniarum**: ' our whole system of credit and finance '.

l. 32. **in foro**: The banks, *tabernae argentariorum*, were in the Forum (the *clivus argentarius*, named after them, runs out of it past the Capitol). The point is that not only private fortunes, but the whole national financial system was at stake.

l. 33. **versatur**: ' is conducted '.

l. 33. **implicata est ... cohaeret**: An attempt might be made to reproduce in English the root meanings of these words. Note the different tenses.

l. 34. **illa**: Neuter although strictly referring to **pecuniae Asiaticae.** Not **haec,** because although referred to last they are geographically the more distant; **haec** is finance at Rome.

l. 34. **ut . . . non**: See note above. **non** qualifies **concidant.**

l. 35. **motu**: In the particular sense of ' political movement ' and so in a bad sense ' rebellion ', ' tumult '.

l. 35. **Quare videte**: This sentence recapitulates the four points of the last four chapters: 1. Rome's good name. 2. Her allies' safety. 3. Her revenues. 4. Her citizens' fortunes.

l. 36. **vobis**: Dative of agent.

Sections 20–21

VIII. 20. line 1. **Quoniam**: Temporal rather than causal. ' Having spoken . . .' rather than ' Since I have spoken . . .'.

l. 1. **de magnitudine**: Cicero now passes to the second main part of his speech. The sheer size of the war demands every effort that the Roman people can expend upon it.

l. 2. **dicam**: Future indicative.

l. 2. **dici**: i.e. by the opponents of strenuous action.

l. 3. **ita . . . ut**: Consecutive. **bellum** should be supplied from **belli genus** as the subject of **sit gerendum.** The two parallel **ita . . . ut** constructions should not be so translated in English. It is better to make the first subordinate, e.g. ' While the nature of the war is so . . . yet it is not . . .'.

l. 4. **In quo . . . est**: ' And in connexion with this point it is my most important task . . .'.

l. 5. **ea . . . videantur**: The neuter pronouns of Latin with verbal adjectives in agreement are best translated by abstract nouns containing the verbal idea: ' lest that foresight which ought to be your major concern become an object of your contempt '.

l. 7. **L. Lucullo**: Cicero is now a member of the Senate by virtue of the quaestorship which he had held in 75. He had attained this office with the support of those whom he had helped in the Courts and the approval of the Optimates. He must therefore tread warily to avoid making too many enemies and endangering his own political future.

The Optimates were strongly opposed to this bill and Lucullus would bitterly resent Pompey's succession to his command. Cicero therefore gives high praise to Lucullus in this section, yet goes on to explain that the magnitude of the task ahead requires the appointment of Pompey.

This section must be read in conjunction with 51 f., pp. 23–25, where he praises the optimate leaders Catulus and Hortensius, yet asserts that events proved them wrong in their opposition to Pompey's earlier command and reaffirms the necessity of appointing Pompey to take over the war against Mithridates.

l. 7. **tantum ... laudis, ...:** 'as much praise as ...'. Partitive genitive.

l. 8. **viro ... homini: viro** = man as opposed to woman and therefore brave; **homini** = man as opposed to animal and therefore having intelligence. Translate **viro** here as ' soldier '.

l. 9. **debeatur:** ' is owed '. Subjunctive because it is the verb of a subordinate clause in indirect speech.

l. 9. **dico:** ' I assert ', ' I maintain '.

l. 9. **adventu:** Temporal: ' at the time of his arrival '.

l. 9. **maximas:** Ancient authorities mention figures of about 150,000 infantry, and between 10,000 and 20,000 cavalry.

l. 10. **ornatas atque instructas fuisse:** This infinitive represents the pluperfect indicative of direct speech. The two verbs are combined to convey the perfection of the equipment of Mithridates' armies.

l. 12. **obsessam esse:** Represents an imperfect indicative ' was invested '.

l. 12. **Cyzicenorum:** This siege became a byword for the heroic resistance of the inhabitants, and the variety of Mithridates' appliances. Cyzicus (see frontispiece map) was one of the leading cities of Asia and was made a *libera civitas* (i.e. independent) by Rome in repayment for its loyalty during the war with Mithridates.

l. 14. **virtute,** . . . **consilio:** Instrumental ablatives. **periculis** is an ablative of separation. These two uses represent the existence of separate cases in the parent language from which Latin is derived.

21. line 16. **classem:** After his retreat from Cyzicus in 73, Mithridates embarked 10,000 men in a fleet of 50 ships led by M. Marius, who had been sent to join him by Sertorius — hence **ducibus Sertorianis.** Lucullus met and destroyed this force in two battles off the Aegean islands of Tenedos and Lemnos. See frontispiece map.

l. 17. **studio atque odio:** ' with the hatred born of civil strife '.

l. 17. **raperetur:** ' was hurrying '.

l. 20. **Pontum:** The kingdom of Pontus, not the Black Sea.

l. 21. **ex omni aditu clausus:** ' barred from all access '.

l. 21. **Sinopen:** Greek form of the accusative of Sinope, by origin a Greek colony, the capital and birthplace of Mithridates.

l. 22. **Amisum:** Another Greek colony, some hundred miles to the east of Sinope, also on the Black Sea coast.

l. 22. **erant:** Indicative because this relative clause is inserted by Cicero, and is not part of the indirect speech.

l. 23. **ceterasque** . . . **permultas:** This phrase must be taken as a whole ' and all the numerous other cities of Pontus and Cappadocia '.

l. 24. **uno:** ' mere '. A rhetorical exaggeration. Their reduction took longer than a year.

l. 25. **alios** . . . **reges:** Firstly to his son-in-law Tigranes, king of Armenia, and his son Machares, ruler of the kingdom of the Bosporus; then to Arsaces, king of Parthia.

l. 27. **salvis** . . . **sociis:** Without imposing forced exactions upon the provincials.

l. 27. **integris vectigalibus:** Without damaging the revenues — to the satisfaction and profit of the *publicani*.

l. 28. **laudis:** Partitive genitive with **satis.**

l. 29. **atque ita:** sc. **dictum.**

l. 30. **obtrectant:** Indicative because the statement is specific not generic, i.e. ' the opponents '. Cf. note on 14, **exportantur,** p. 51.

l. 31. **hoc loco:** The Rostra.

Sections 22–26

IX. 22. line 1. **Requiretur:** Impersonal passive introducing a possible objection.

l. 5. **Medea illa:** ' Medea in the story '. The daughter of Aeetes, king of Colchis, who fell in love with Jason, the leader of the Argonauts, and helped him obtain the Golden Fleece. In their subsequent flight from Colchis she murdered her brother Absyrtus and scattered the fragments in the sea in order that her father might stop to pick them up and thus be delayed in his pursuit.

l. 7. **se:** Refers, as we should expect, to Medea, the subject of the main verb.

Notice the rhetorical language of this sentence: **eorum collectio dispersa,** ' the picking up of the scattered pieces ', **maeror patrius.**

l. 9. **Sic Mithridates:** This sentence has the normal Latin word-order which ensures that its sense is not complete until the final stop. This order must be altered to ensure an idiomatic translation.

l. 11. **maioribus:** ' ancestors '.

l. 12. **bello superiore:** The First Mithridatic War, 88–84.

l. 13. **Haec dum . . .:** Note word-order.

l. 15. **Ita illum:** This contrast makes a neat ending to the story. **illum** is Aeetes, **hos** the troops of Lucullus.

23. line 16. **illo:** Agreeing with the nearer noun only. Translate: ' a terrified fugitive '.

l. 17. **diffidentemque . . . adflictum . . . perditumque:** We should probably translate these participles by nouns or short clauses, e.g. **diffidentemque . . . confirmavit:** ' gave him new strength in his despair '.

l. 20. **plures . . . gentes:** In his *Life of Lucullus,* Plutarch gives a list of the eastern nations now raised against Rome;

among them the Medes, Arabs, and various Caspian tribes. Plutarch of Chaeronea, who lived *c.* A.D. 46–*c.* 120, was a Greek biographer and moral philosopher who wrote a series of *Parallel Lives* comparing the lives of pairs of eminent Greeks and Romans. He was concerned to bring out the moral character of his subject rather than to relate him to the political background of his time, but included a host of anecdotes which help to fill in our knowledge of the history of the times.

l. 22. **nationibus**: This word usually refers to peoples felt to be less civilized than the Romans.

l. 23. **lacessendas bello**: i.e. by hostile acts to incite the other side to open war.

l. 23. **temptandas**: ' disturb ', ' interfere with '.

l. 24. **gravis ... opinio**: ' a strong and most important belief '.

l. 25. **fani**: Probably a temple in the region of the Euphrates (modern Luristan), which was subject to periodic attacks by the Syrians and Parthians.

l. 26. **religiosissimi**: ' extremely holy '.

l. 28. **multae atque magnae**: When **multus** and another positive adjective qualify the same noun, they must be joined by a conjunction which should be omitted when translating into English.

l. 29. **urbem**: Tigranocerta.

l. 30. **Tigrani regno**: Armenia. **ex** avoids two genitives and may be meant to denigrate the achievement of Lucullus ' out of the whole of Tigranes's kingdom '.

l. 30. **usus erat**: ' had experienced '.

l. 31. **nimia longinquitate**: Cicero does not say that the army was in open mutiny in order to spare the feelings of his audience.

l. 31. **desiderio suorum**: ' a longing for home '.

24. line 32. **Hic ... dicam**: To avoid mentioning the mutiny.

l. 33. **fuit ... extremum**: ' for the end of the matter was that ...'. **ut** is consecutive.

l. 37. **hoc fere sic fieri solere**: ' that it almost always happens that '.

l. 38. **ut:** ' so that '.

l. 39. **multorum . . . ad misericordiam:** ' move many power-ful men to pity '.

l. 41. **nomen regale:** ' the name of king '.

25. line 42. **tantum . . . quantum:** English would use a comparative phrase followed by the positive adverb and the verb in the conditional mood: ' more than he would ever have dared expect before his defeat '.

l. 44. **eo contentus, . . . acciderat:** This is explained by the following **ut** clause which is in apposition.

l. 45. **illam . . . terram:** His kingdom.

l. 45. **pulsus erat:** Pluperfect rather than the more usual perfect, because only by using this tense can the priority be expressed, since the main verb is itself pluperfect.

l. 47. **victorem:** Used as an adjective.

l. 47. **impetum fecit:** In 67 C. Triarius was utterly defeated at the Battle of Zela with the loss of 7,000 men and his camp taken.

l. 48. **poetae:** The two best-known are Cn. Naevius (*c.* 270–201), who wrote in Saturnian metre a history of the rise of Rome and of the First Punic War, and Q. Ennius (239–169), ' the father of Roman poetry ', who wrote an epic in eighteen books of hexameters — the *Annales* — recounting Roman history down to 171.

l. 48. **res Romanas:** ' Roman history '.

l. 50. **non ex proelio:** Lucullus, who was advancing from Mesopotamia to the Euphrates, heard the news of the disaster from the local inhabitants, not from messengers of Triarius.

l. 51. **sermone:** A talking with anyone, so ' conversation '.

26. line 52. **belli offensione:** ' defeat in battle '.

l. 52. **tamen:** i.e. in spite of the disaster.

l. 53. **aliqua ex parte:** ' to some extent '.

l. 53. **incommodis:** The neuter plural of the adjective used as a noun. ' losses '.

l. 55. **vetere exemplo:** As a counter-balance to the almost unlimited extent of the power enjoyed by a holder of the *imperium*, the Roman constitution had ensured that the tenure of the power should be short. But with the increasing complexity of Rome's overseas commitments the necessity of longer commands had been appreciated, and by this time it was the established practice to allow a successful general to complete his campaign. Lucullus had enjoyed such an extended command which was only brought to an end by political intrigues and animosities at Rome.

l. 56. **stipendiis confectis:** '[men] who had served their time'. Lit. 'with completed campaigns'. An ablative of description or quality. An ablative noun with an epithet may be attached to another noun to describe it. This use arose from the case denoting attendant circumstances, and developed in such a way that the ablative words could be used either attributively or (as here) predicatively like any other adjective.

l. 56. **M'. Glabrioni:** Consul in 67 and proconsul in Bithynia and Pontus the following year.

l. 57. **ea:** Neuter plural referring to **multa.**

l. 58. **coniectura:** Instrumental ablative ' by means of '.

l. 58. **quantum ... putetis:** ' the size of a war '. **factum putetis,** cf. note on 11, **videte ... putetis,** p. 46.

l. 59. **coniungant:** ' fight in concert '. The mood of the verb in this relative clause indicates its causal force.

l. 60. **integrae:** i.e. previously untouched by war.

l. 60. **novus imperator:** Glabrio.

Sections 27-28

X. 27. line 6. **innocentium:** ' honest '. Cf. use of **innocentia** in 36, p. 17.

l. 6. **copiam:** ' supply '.

l. 9. **unus:** ' alone '.

l. 10. **antiquitatis memoriam:** i.e. those of the past whom we remember.

l. 11. **virtute:** ' in merit '.

28. line 14. **res:** ' qualities '.

l. 15. **virtutem:** A difficult word to translate. It means professional ability rather than merely soldierly courage.   See 29 ff., p. 14, for what Cicero had in his mind.

l. 15. **auctoritatem:** Most important for a Roman public figure; ' prestige '. See note on 1, **auctoritatem**, p. 35.

l. 15. **felicitatem:** Another quality more important in Roman eyes. See note on 10, **felicitati**, p. 45.

l. 15. **Quis . . . scientior:** =*Cui plus scientiae fuit.*

l. 17. **e ludo . . . disciplinis:** ' after his schooling and the studies of boyhood '.

l. 17. **bello maximo . . . profectus est:** In the fighting against the Marsi during the Social War. We have an inscription showing that in 89 he was a member of the *consilium* or staff of his father, Cn. Pompeius Strabo, who, as one of the consuls of that year, was the Roman commander in this campaign. There was bitter fighting, and the epithet **acerrimis** is well deserved. The ablatives **bello** and **hostibus** are ablatives of attendant circumstances, one of a number of uses of this case, deriving from the assumption of the functions of a case which had existed separately at an earlier stage of linguistic development, and had expressed the idea of accompaniment.

l. 19. **extrema pueritia:** Born in 106, he was seventeen years old in the campaign of 89, and still only nineteen when a member of his father's army fighting Cinna.

l. 21. **exercitus imperator:** On Sulla's return to Italy from Greece in 83 Pompey joined the Sullan party, and in Picenum raised an army of three legions for him.

l. 22. **quisquam:** ' any other single individual '.

l. 22. **concertavit:** Particularly of legal disputes. A *hostis* is a public enemy and an *inimicus* private.

l. 24. **provincias:** Here used in its original meaning ' sphere of administration ', ' office '. The word at first meant the sphere of action of a magistrate possessing *imperium* and later, with Roman expansion overseas, came to denote the geographical area over which the magistrate had control.

l. 26. **suis:** Because the grammatical subject **adulescentia** implies the *adulescens*, Pompey.

l. 26. **offensionibus:** See note on 26, **belli offensione,** p. 60.

l. 27. **triumphis**: He had already celebrated two triumphs — over the Marians in 79, and after the Servile War in 71.

l. 29. **exercuerit**: A consecutive perfect subjunctive.

l. 29. **fortuna**: ' misfortune '.

l. 29. **Civile**: Against Cinna, Carbo and Lepidus. **Africanum**, against the Marian remnants in Africa. **Transalpinum**, against Gallic tribes on his way to fight Sertorius in Spain in 76. **Hispaniense**, against Sertorius. **servile**, against the slaves in their uprising in 71 on his return from Spain. **navale**, against the pirates in 67.

l. 33. **in usu positam militari**: ' within the range of military experience '. **esse** is not to be taken with **positam**.

Sections 29–30

XI. 29. line 1. **Iam vero**: ' Moreover '. These words emphasize the transition to a still more important theme, Pompey's military capacity.

l. 3. **cuiquam**: Dative of the agent with the perfect participle passive.

l. 4. **virtutes imperatoriae**: ' the qualities necessary in a general '.

l. 5. **labor**: ' energy '.

l. 7. **tanta . . . quanta**: See note on 25, **tantum . . . quantum**, p. 60.

30. line 10. **Italia**: After the return of Sulla from the East in 83. See 28 above, p. 13.

l. 11. **Sicilia**: Late in 82 Pompey crossed to Sicily, and the Marian opposition disintegrated without serious fighting. Their leader, the consul Cn. Papirius Carbo, was caught on the island of Pantellaria and executed.

l. 12. **terrore . . . celeritate**: A neat example of chiasmus.

l. 13. **explicavit**: ' released ', ' extricated '.

l. 13. **Africa, . . . Gallia, . . . Hispania, . . . Italia**: See 28, above, and Introduction, pp. xxxix–xl.

l. 20. **cum**: A conjunction.

l. 20. **bello taetro periculosoque**: Cicero had good cause to apply such words to the rising of the slaves under Spartacus.

The political upheavals of the past decades had seen the recruitment of slaves by political leaders for use against Roman citizens, but for the past hundred years and more the economic development of the Sicilian and Italian countryside had tended to concentrate potential rebels in increasing numbers. Sicily, after suffering sporadic outbreaks from the middle of the second century B.C. onwards, had witnessed in 135 the outbreak of the First Servile War which ravaged the island and only after three years' hard fighting was it successfully ended by a consul of the year, P. Rupilius. 104 saw the outbreak of the Second Servile War which again brought bitter fighting to the fields of Sicily; not that Italy herself was free from minor revolts throughout this period, but they were kept in check and remained small.

The first century B.C. saw both Marius and Sulla enrolling slaves to take part in the internecine strife against free-born Romans who were their political opponents. It was in 73, however, that Rome, was confronted by the most serious situation that she had ever had to face in Italy. Under the leadership of the Thracian gladiator Spartacus, the slaves defeated one of the praetors and made themselves masters of southern Italy. In the following year they defeated two consular armies and the proconsul of Cisalpine Gaul, but the Senate then appointed M. Licinius Crassus, one of the praetors of this year, as its commander and he swiftly brought the war to a successful end. The serious fighting was over when Pompey arrived on the scene, and his part in the war was confined to rounding up defeated fugitives.

l. 21. **absente**: When the participle is used as an adjective the ablative ends in -*i*, when as a noun or verb (in the ablative absolute construction) in -*e*.

l. 22. **attenuatum ... ac sepultum**: See above note. There is no justification for Cicero's claim.

Sections 31–35

31. line 1. **nunc vero iam**: A very emphatic transitional phrase to introduce the climax of this account of the campaigns of Pompey, the Pirate War.

l. 2. **maria ... universa**: ' the high seas '.

l. 3. **tum:** ' as well as '.

l. 3. **in singulis oris:** ' along the various shores '.

l. 6. **ut lateret?:** ' as to escape notice '.

l. 7. **cum . . . navigaret?:** ' since he had to sail '.

l. 8. **hieme:** Mediterranean navigation usually ceased during the winter (cf. Acts xxvii. 9 ff.), and the pirates could be expected not to put to sea in the winter months. But we hear from Dio Cassius (c. A.D. 150–235), who wrote a history of Rome, that not even were the winter months safe from their depredations.

l. 8. **referto praedonum:** This genitive with words denoting fullness or abundance is partitive in origin.

l. 9. **turpe:** See 33 below, pp. 15–16, for the sort of thing that was happening.

l. 10. **ab omnibus . . . imperatore:** This is a very strained use of the rhetorical figure of speech known as *commutatio*: ' You must eat to live, not live to eat '. **omnibus imperatoribus:** all living Roman commanders. **omnibus annis:** their whole life.

32. **line 14. vectigal:** Note how early this comes in Cicero's list. Cf. note on 14, **praesertim cum,** p. 50, and other passages which show the importance of the Romans' financial stake in the provinces.

l. 15. **classibus vestris:** Instrumental ablative.

l. 16. **quam multas . . . captas urbes:** Plutarch in his *Life of Pompey* gives the figure as 400.

XII. **line 18. longinqua:** ' distant events '.

l. 18. **Fuit:** The perfect tense indicates a past state which has now ceased to exist.

l. 19. **longe a domo:** It is Cicero's practice to use the accusative and ablative cases without prepositions to indicate motion to or from a point when that point is indicated by the name of a town or small island, or by the words *domus, rus,* and *humus.* The preposition, however, is used in certain circumstances and is regularly found in conjunction with *longe.* In later prose writers from Livy onwards it is often found in any circumstances.

l. 20. **propugnaculis imperii:** ' with the bulwarks of empire '. Her armies and fleets.

l. 22. **dicam:** Deliberative subjunctive. ' Am I to say . . .'.

l. 22. **vestri**: Rather than **nostri** to bring home to his audience that these armies were their own responsibility.

l. 23. **Brundisio**: The shortest sea crossing was from Brundisium which was therefore the most usual port of embarkation for Greece.

l. 25. **redempti sint?**: ' have been ransomed '. We know of no corroboration for this story, but there is no good reason to doubt it.

l. 27. **duodecim secures**: ' two praetors '. An example of metonomy, a figure of speech in which an attribute is substituted for the thing or person intended. Although a praetor had only two lictors in Rome, he had six in the provinces and the lictors only carried their axes outside the city. Plutarch tells us that their names were Sextilius and Bellinus, but we do not know anything more about them.

33. line 28. **Cnidum** . . .: Plutarch confirms the story of these attacks.

l. 31. **quibus**: Instrumental ablative.

l. 31. **vitam et spiritum**: Probably a reference to the imports of corn which were seriously disrupted by the pirates. See 34, p. 16.

l. 32. **An . . . ignoratis**: ' Do you really not know . . .? '

l. 32. **Caietae**: On the coast of Latium. See map, pp. viii and ix. Note the genitive of definition. It is more usual to find the place-name in apposition to the common noun, and therefore in the same case.

l. 33. **celeberrimum**: ' very busy '.

l. 33. **inspectante**: cf. note on 30, **absente**, p. 64.

l. 34. **praetore**: Possibly M. Antonius Creticus, who was praetor in 74 and in command of a fleet to deal with the pirates, and we read in Plutarch that a daughter of his father M. Antonius (cf. **liberos** below, a rhetorical plural as **duces** in 9, p. 44 for Sertorius), was captured on the coast of Italy.

l. 36. **Nam**: Omit in translation. It merely connects this sentence with what has gone before.

l. 37. **Ostiense**: This is confirmed by Dio Cassius.

l. 37. **incommodum**: ' reverse ', ' set-back '.

l. 37. **labem**: ' stain ', ' blot '. Cf. **macula**.

l. 38. **prope inspectantibus vobis**: ' almost before your very eyes '. Ostia at the mouth of the Tiber was only some sixteen miles from Rome.

l. 40. **praepositus esset**: The subjunctive has consecutive force. Translate ' a fleet important enough to be commanded by a consul of the Roman people ' not ' a fleet which had a consul of the Roman people in command '.

l. 40. **oppressa est?** Indicative because the *cum*-clause identifies the **Ostiense incommodum** by indicating an action which is its equivalent.

l. 41. **Pro**: An exclamation, also spelt **proh**.

l. 41. **hominis**: Not **viri** because his **virtus** ' genius ' is **divina** and is being contrasted with that of mere mortals.

l. 43. **modo**: ' only recently '.

l. 45. **Oceani ostium**: The Strait of Gibraltar.

34. line 46. **Atque haec . . .**: Watch the order of the sentence in translation.

l. 47. **a me**: This ablative of the agent with the preposition is occasionally found instead of the dative of the agent with the gerundive although there is no ambiguity involved such as there is in the case of 6, **a vobis**. (See note *ad loc.*, p. 41.)

l. 47. **praetereunda**: Attracted into the plural to agree with **haec** instead of the expected **praetereundum non est**. Cicero is not recounting the feats of Pompey but their speed.

l. 51. **tanti . . . navigavit?**: ' this mighty wave of war swept over the sea '. Figurative for the huge fleet of Pompey.

l. 52. **nondum . . . mari**: See note on 31, **hieme**, p. 65. See also 35, **ineunte vere**, p. 17.

l. 54. **haec . . . subsidia**: ' these three sources of the corn supply '.

35. line 56. **duabus Hispaniis**: *Citerior* and *Ulterior*, Nearer and Further.

l. 56. **Gallia Transalpina**: The southern part of Gaul became a Roman province in 122. Hence *Provincia* gave its name to Provence.

l. 57. **confirmata**: Agrees with **Gallia,** the nearest noun, but refers to **Hispaniis** as well.

l. 58. **oram Illyrici maris**: The Illyrian shore of the Adriatic Sea.

l. 58. **Achaiam omnemque Graeciam**: Cicero uses this phrase because Achaia refers to the Peloponnese only and is not yet in current use for the whole of Greece.

l. 59. **Italiae duo maria**: The *Mare Hadriaticum* or *Superum* and the *Mare Tyrrhenum* or *Inferum*.

l. 60. **ut**: ' from the time when '.

l. 63. **ubique**: ' wherever they were '.

l. 63. **praedones**: The antecedent has been attracted into the relative clause, as often happens, particularly when it has an epithet, or is in apposition to another noun.

l. 65. **Cretensibus**: See 46, p. 21. Driven by the cruelty of Q. Metellus. This discreditable affair nearly caused an outbreak of fighting between two Roman commanders.

l. 65. **usque in Pamphyliam**: Cicero makes his point by a piece of rhetorical trickery. His audience in far away Rome would not realise that Pamphylia is in comparison no great distance from Crete. For this dative, see note on 10, **ei**, p. 46.

l. 66. **deprecatoresque**: = *ad deprecandum,* ' envoys to plead their cause '.

l. 67. **obsidesque**: As a mark of clemency, that they might hope for his protection. A negative sentence is commonly followed by *et, -que* or *ac*. Translate ' but '.

l. 67. **imperavit**: is followed by the accusative of the thing demanded.

l. 68. **tam diuturnum**: See note on 11, **saepe ... gesserunt**, p. 46.

l. 71. **confecit**: The whole campaign lasted only three months. It took forty days to clear the western Mediterranean and then a further forty-nine to deal with the East.

Section 36

XIII. 36. line 1. **virtus imperatoris**: ' genius as a general '.

l. 2. **ceterae**: The moral and intellectual qualities required.

l. 2. **paulo ante:** In 29, p. 14.

l. 5. **artes:** ' qualities '. This word means something not very different from **virtutes** but implies their practical operation.

l. 6. **huius:** i.e. **bellandi virtus.**

l. 6. **administrae:** Lit. ' helper '. Translate by a relative clause.

l. 7. **innocentia:** Ablative. See note on 26, **stipendiis confectis,** p. 61. Translate by ' integrity '. 37–39, pp. 17–18, below make this quality clear. See also 61, p. 28.

l. 9. **facilitate:** ' graciousness ', ' affability '. It is the readiness to listen to others.

l..9. **humanitate:** ' courtesy '. Cf. 41, **faciles aditus,** p. 19.

l. 10. **quae . . . consideremus:** ' Let us briefly consider their nature as found in Cn. Pompeius '.

l. 11. **summa:** ' in the highest degree '.

l. 12. **contentione:** ' comparison '.

Sections 37–39

37. line 1. **ullo in numero putare:** Lit. ' to reckon in any number ' (of generals), i.e. to count as a general at all.

l. 2. **veneant atque venierint?:** Used as the passive of **vendo.** The reverse order of tenses would be the more natural in English.

l. 3. **quid . . . cogitare:** To be taken closely together. **hunc hominem** is the subject of **cogitare** which to be constructed after the **possumus . . . putare** of the previous sentence.

l. 4. **aerario:** The public treasury. The governor of a province was not paid but received money from the treasury at Rome to cover his expenses.

l. 5. **propter cupiditatem provinciae:** This must mean ' ambition to retain his province ' rather than ' obtain a province '.

l. 7. **in quaestu:** ' on loan '.

l. 8. **admurmuratio:** The sentence makes it clear that this word means a noise of disapproval of the men about whom Cicero has been talking rather than one of approval of his words.

l. 10. **ante:** Here the adverb.

l. 10. **voluerit:** Future perfect.

l. 12. **calamitates:** ' ruin '.

l. 13. **ferant:** ' bring in their train ', not ' suffer '.

38. line 13. **Itinera:** Before **quae** for emphasis. The mood shows that **quae** is interrogative, not relative.

l. 14. **civium Romanorum:** The Italians had received full Roman citizenship after the Social War.

l. 17. **existimetis:** See note on 11, **videte . . . putetis,** p. 46.

l. 18. **hibernis:** One of the heavy obligations laid upon towns in the provinces was the provision of winter-quarters for the Roman troops. Wealthy towns often purchased exemption — a fruitful source of enrichment to a governor. One of the advantages enjoyed by *civitates liberae* was freedom from this burden.

39. line 22. **Hic:** ' in these circumstances '.

l. 24. **non modo . . . dicatur?:** The second **non** after the **modo** is regularly omitted when there is a predicate common to both clauses, so that the negative in **ne . . . quidem** can be referred to the whole sentence. Cicero means that far from ravaging the country, they kept to a minimum the damage done by their march through it.

l. 26. **Iam vero:** See note on these words at the beginning of 29, p. 63.

l. 27. **sermones:** i.e. by word of mouth.

l. 29. **Hiemis . . . avaritiae:** ' from the winter . . . for avarice '. Note the change from the objective to subjective genitive. Cf. note on 44, **unius hominis spe ac nomine,** p. 73.

l. 30. **sociorum atque amicorum:** See note on 4, **sociis,** p. 37.

Sections 40–42

XIV. 40. line 1. **Age vero:** The singular is used, even to large audiences, because the phrase had become stereotyped and almost the equivalent of a transitional particle.

l. 2. **Unde . . . inventum:** ' How do you think he acquired that great speed . . .'.

l. 4. **inaudita:** ' hitherto unknown '.

l. 7. **non avaritia ...**: Owing to his **innocentia**.

l. 8. **devocavit**: ' called off ', ' allured '.

l. 9. **amoenitas**: In classical authors this word always refers to the beauty of nature.

l. 10. **nobilitas**: ' renown '. Plutarch in his *Life of Pompey* tells us that not even Athens detained him for long.

l. 11. **labor**: ' energy '.

l. 11. **signa ... arbitrantur**: Roman officials were accomplished looters of works of art, and many a noble house in Rome came to be decorated with the works of Greek artists.   The best-known account in Latin literature of this sort of behaviour is contained in Cicero's speeches against Verres, the infamous and rapacious propraetor of Sicily from 73 to 71.

41. line 16. delapsum: The verb **delabor** is regularly used of the descent of gods to earth.

l. 17. **fuisse**: Note the position of this word in the sentence. ' that there really were ... '.

l. 17. **quondam**: This goes with **continentia** not **fuisse**. Translate ' who once showed such self-control '.

l. 18. **quod iam ... videbatur**: ' which was beginning to seem '; **falso memoriae proditum**, lit. ' falsely handed down to memory '; translate ' a complete myth '.

l. 22. **cum ... habebamus**: The indicative is here used in a *cum*-clause in past time because the clause merely identifies the time of their preference.

l. 24. **Iam vero**: ' Furthermore '.

l. 24. **faciles aditus**: cf. note on 36, **facilitate**, p. 69.

l. 24. **privatorum**: Private individuals as opposed to magistrates.

l. 25. **liberae**: ' without restriction '.

l. 25. **de aliorum iniuriis**: ' about wrongs done them by others '.   A subjective genitive.

l. 26. **dignitate**: ' rank '.   An ablative of respect.   It is uncertain whether this example is a locative or instrumental use in origin.

42. line 27. consilio: Political wisdom.

l. 28. **gravitate:** ' dignity '. A quality highly prized by the Romans.

l. 28. **copia:** ' fluency '.

l. 28. **valeat:** Pompey is the subject.

l. 28. **in quo ipso: dicendi** is the antecedent.

l. 29. **quaedam dignitas imperatoria:** ' something of the authority appropriate to a general '.

l. 29. **hoc ipso ex loco:** The Rostra. (And without the need of moving from it.)

l. 30. **Fidem:** ' word of honour '.

l. 32. **sanctissimam:** ' completely inviolable '.

l. 32. **Humanitate ... mansuetudinem:** We know that he showed a prudent clemency towards many of the surrendered pirates, and this in all probability influenced the Cretans who wished to surrender to him rather than to Q. Metellus. In 46 below, however, Cicero attributes their behaviour to the prestige of Pompey. **virtutem:** Here ' bravery '.

l. 35. **quisquam ... quin:** These words are used because of the negative force of the rhetorical question.

l. 37. **ad ... conficienda:** ' to end all the wars of our time '. **ad** with the gerundive is regularly used to express purpose.

Sections 43-45

XV. 43. line 1. **auctoritas:** The third qualification of a great general: ' prestige '. See note on 1, **auctoritatem**, p. 35.

l. 3. **ea re:** sc. *auctoritate.* This is the main basis for opposition to the *lex Manilia.*

l. 4. **Vehementer ... pertinere:** The object of **ignorat.** Vehementer, ' very greatly ', ' that it is most important '.

l. 7. **aut contemnant aut metuant:** These verbs refer to the feelings of the enemy; **aut oderint aut ament** to those of the allies.

l. 8. **opinione:** What is being generally said or thought.

l. 9. **aliqua ratione certa:** ' any rational process of thought '.

l. 13. **iudicia:** ' marks of esteem ' by election to high offices and important commands.

44. line 14. **quo**: 'whither'; =**ut eo,** and the subjunctive is con secutive.

l. 14. **illius diei**: On which the *lex Gabinia* had given Pompey command in the war against the pirates.

l. 16. **templis**: The Forum was overlooked by the temples of Vesta and Castor on the Palatine, and of Saturn and Concordia on the Capitoline.

l. 17. **unum**: 'alone'.

l. 18. **ut plura non dicam**: 'without saying more'. Consecutive not final, and therefore **ut . . . non . . . neque. . . .**

l. 20. **auctoritas**: Prestige in general.

l. 21. **omnium rerum egregiarum**: 'of every kind of distinction'.

l. 22. **qui quo die**: English does not use the double relative. Translate 'for on the day on which he . . .'.

l. 23. **vilitas annonae**: 'fall in the price of corn'.

l. 23. **ex summa inopia et caritate**: We should say 'after a time of . . .'.

l. 24. **unius hominis spe ac nomine**: **hominis** is an objective genitive after **spe,** but a possessive when taken with **nomine.** Cf. note on 39, **Hiemis . . . avaritiae,** p. 70.

45. line 27. **calamitate**: See Introduction, p. xxviii, and 25, p. 12.

l. 27. **de quo . . . admonui**: 'to which I reluctantly referred you . . .'.

l. 28. **pertimuissent**: The prefix *per-* strengthens the meaning of the simple verb.

l. 29. **animique**: 'spirit', 'resolution'.

l. 31. **discrimen**: 'the critical moment'.

l. 31. **divinitus**: 'providentially'.

l. 32. **fortuna populi Romani**: The war against the pirates had taken Pompey to Asia Minor. Cf. 50, p. 23.

l. 33. **adventus**: 'mere arrival', as in 13 and 15, pp. 6 and 7.

l. 33. **insolita**: Admittedly Sulla and Murena had been awarded triumphs over him and he could be said to be accustomed to defeat at the hands of Lucullus, but see 8, p. 4, which suggests that Cicero is not wholly accurate in the impression he conveys.

l. 34. **inflatum**: ' elated '.

l. 34. **continuit . . . retardavit**: ' halted ' the immediate, and ' kept back ' the distant enemy.

l. 38. **ipso**: ' mere '.

l. 39. **rumore**: ' reputation '.

Section 46

XVI. 46. line 1. **Age vero**: See note on 40, p. 70.

l. 1. **illa res**: Refers to **quod . . . dediderunt.**

l. 2. **auctoritatem**: Cicero is not justified in ascribing these happenings to the prestige of Pompey, but it improves his case to do so.

l. 3. **diversis**: ' different '.

l. 5. **noster imperator**: Q. Metellus.

l. 6. **in ultimas prope terras**: ' almost to the ends of the earth '. In fact Pamphylia. See 35, p. 17.

l. 9. **usque in Hispaniam**: We know from other sources that Mithridates entered into negotiations with Pompey's opponent, Sertorius, in 75 and in the following year made a formal treaty with him. There is no independent support for this story which appears to have been current in two versions; one — Pompey's — that Mithridates entered into negotiations with Pompey by means of an envoy, preferring him to the original commander of the war against Sertorius, Q. Metellus Pius; and one — that of Metellus to whom it was **molestum** that a mere quaestor had been preferred to a consular — that the alleged envoy was in fact a spy and the tale of his mission a ' cover story ' prepared against the possibility of capture.

l. 11. **ii**: Particularly Metellus.

l. 11. **molestum**: ' annoying '.

l. 11. **ad eum potissimum**: ' to him rather than to others '.

l. 15. **iudiciis**: cf. note on 43, **iudicia**, p. 72.

Sections 47–48

47. line 1. **Reliquum est . . .:** Take this sentence in the order: **Reliquum est ut . . . dicamus de felicitate quam . . . possumus, sicut . . . deorum.**

l. 1. **praestare:** ' guarantee '.

l. 3. **aequum est:** sc. *dicere*.

l. 3. **potestate:** ' what is within the power of . . .'.

l. 5. **Maximo, Marcello, Scipioni, Mario:** Q. Fabius Maximus Cunctator as dictator and consul contained Hannibal in Italy during the Second Punic War; M. Claudius Marcellus was another consular commander against Hannibal, and captured Syracuse after a long siege in 212; P. Scipio Aemilianus the Younger finally destroyed Carthage in 146 at the end of the Third Punic War, and was the captor of Numantia in Spain in 133; Gaius Marius, who turned the Roman army into a professional fighting force, defeated Jugurtha, king of Numidia in 105, and the Gallic peoples, the Teutoni and Cimbri, in 102 and 101.

l. 13. **non ut . . . sed ut:** Consecutive, looking back to **hac.**

l. 15. **invisa . . . ingrata:** ' causing offence ' because **fortuna** is not **in illius potestate** but in that of the gods; ' ungrateful ' because such an assumption ignores the kindness and bounty of the gods.

48. line 16. **non sum praedicaturus:** The rhetorical device of *praeteritio* in which you tell your audience what you are not going to say to them. Cf. 60, **Non dicam,** p. 28.

l. 19. **adsenserint:** Normally used by Cicero in the passive form.

l. 21. **hoc:** ' this one point '.

l. 23. **tacitus:** ' in his heart '. The addition of this word makes the assertion more telling because many express silent wishes for more than they would dare to hope aloud.

l. 24. **detulerunt: Defero** means ' I give without being asked '.

l. 25. **proprium:** ' assured '.

Sections 49–50

49. line 1. **Quare:** This section recapitulates the whole case.

l. 2. **accuratissime:** The force of **cura** is stronger than anything suggested by our derived word *accurate*. Translate ' with the most scrupulous care '.

l. 5. **dubitatis:** ' do you hesitate to . . .'. In this sense it is more normally followed by the infinitive.

l. 6. **hoc tantum boni:** ' this great boon '. Sc. of appointing such a general.

l. 8. **conferatis?:** Contrasted with **detulerunt** above, this verb means that what is being given has been requested.

XVII. 50. line 10. **erat deligendus:** The gerundive with a past tense of the verb *to be* expresses an idea analogous to that of the potential subjunctive in the apodosis of unreal conditions, and the verb therefore regularly remains in the indicative mood.

l. 11. **nunc:** ' but as it is '.

l. 13. **iis qui habent:** Lucullus, Glabrio, and Marcius Rex.

l. 15. **cetera:** sc. *quae communia sunt* rather than *bella*. **summa** is ablative with **salute**.

l. 17. **regium:** ' against a king '; ' this Mithridatic War '.

Section 51

51. line 1. **At enim:** Introducing the objections of his opponents.

l. 1. **rei publicae:** An objective genitive is regularly found with a participle used as an adjective. Cf. Note on 7, **appetentes** p. 42.

l. 2. **beneficiis:** Commonly refers to the higher posts conferred upon a man by popular vote.

l. 2. **Q. Catulus:** Q. Lutatius Catulus, the consul of 78 who had suppressed the rebellion of his colleague Lepidus with the young Pompey's aid, was now recognised as the leader of the conservative party and had opposed the proposals of Gabinius and Manilius. See note on 20, **L. Lucullo**, p. 55.

l. 3. **honoris:** ' high office '. He was consul in 69.

l. 3. **fortunae:** ' wealth '.

l. 3. **virtutis**: His merit in general.

l. 4. **ingenii**: Ability as an orator.

l. 4. **Q. Hortensius**: Q. Hortensius Hortalus was Cicero's chief rival in the law courts. He had defended Verres and became a firm supporter of the senatorial opposition to these tribunician proposals.

l. 5. **multis locis**: ' on many occasions '.

l. 7. **cognoscetis**: See 68, p. 32.

l. 9. **ipsa re ac ratione**: ' from the facts by themselves ' — as opposed to **auctoritatibus**, ' opinions '.

l. 10. **hoc**: An ablative of the measure of difference, in origin an instrumental ablative expressing the amount by which things differ.

l. 11. **isti**: Those opponents upon whose opinions you rely. Cf. the use of **istorum** in 21, p. 10.

l. 13. **summa ... omnia**: ' all the highest qualities '.

Sections 52–53

52. Cicero deals with the question of the command against the pirates at such length because he wants to argue that had the opposition to the *lex Gabinia* been successful, Rome's empire would not have survived, and that the opposition to the *lex Manilia* is equally mistaken. He fails to answer his opponents' point, that there is no good in having the freedom of the seas and peace in the provinces, if you surrender the city's liberty to the rule of one man.

l. 1. **omnia**: The *lex Manilia* would place virtually the whole control of the Roman empire in the hands of Pompey.

l. 2. **sint**: Subjunctive owing to the indirect speech of this passage; it is what Hortensius is reported to have said.

l. 4. **oratio**: ' language '. Cf. this use in 3, p. 37.

l. 4. **re**: ' the facts ', ' the event '.

l. 5. **pro tua ... dicendi**: Hortensius was an exponent of the Asiatic or florid style of oratory. See Introduction, p. xvi. **pro**: ' in accordance with '.

l. 7. **A. Gabinium**: The tribune of 67 who introduced the bill which became the *lex Gabinia de piratis persequendis*.

78   DE IMPERIO CN. POMPEI

l. 9. **promulgasset:** 'had published'.

l. 9. **hoc ipso loco:** The Rostra.

53. line 12. **vera causa:** 'their true interest'.

l. 15. **cum ... capiebantur?:** See 32, p. 15. The mood is indicative because the *cum-* clause identifies the time at which the action of the main verb took place.

l. 16. **ex omnibus provinciis:** We should say 'with' in English, attaching the phrase as the equivalent of an adjective to the noun, instead of making it an adverbial phrase — as all prepositional phrases in Latin must be — qualifying the verb. Cf. note on 13, **adventus in urbes,** p. 49, for an example of Latin deviation from this usage which might well have been extended to this instance, in view of the strong verbal force in the noun **commeatu** 'intercourse'.

l. 19. **obire:** 'transact', 'attend to'.

Sections 54–55

XVIII. 54. line 1. **non dico Atheniensium:** English would not retain these genitives of the inhabitants of the cities, but would substitute the names of the cities themselves in apposition to **civitas.**

l. 2. **quondam:** The Athenian naval empire lasted from the defeat of the second Persian invasion of Greece in 478 to the defeat of Athens by Sparta at the end of the Peloponnesian War in 404. It was at its zenith in the middle of the century.

l. 3. **Carthaginiensium:** These maritime traders of Phoenician origin had in their hey-day won control over the western Mediterranean, a large portion of Sicily, and the mineral and human wealth of Spain.

l. 4. **Rhodiorum:** After the death of Alexander the Great and the division of his empire into three successor states, Rhodes became one of the leading naval powers of the eastern Mediterranean. But after a period as an ally of Rome, she lost Roman support during the second century and her sea-power declined. This decline left a naval vacuum, and was one of the causes which contributed to the growth of piracy.

l. 9. **defenderet:** Note the mood when translating.

l. 9. **continuos**: ' successive ', ' consecutive '.

l. 12. **permanserit**: A perfect subjunctive with consecutive force. ' so strong that it has remained . . .'.

l. 12. **ac**: Introducing a climax. ' great; indeed, by far the greatest part '.

l. 13. **utilitatis**: ' its interests ', i.e. the loss of corn and revenues from taxation.

l. 13. **imperii**: Owing to her inability to protect the provincials and her own magistrates.

55. line 14. **Antiochum**: Antiochus of Syria, against whom the Romans fought from 191 to 187 with their allies Rhodes and Pergamum. C. Livius Salinator defeated his fleet off Corycus in 191, and L. Aemilius Regillus at Myonnesus in 190.

l. 15. **Persemque**: Perseus was the king of Macedonia 179–168, and was Rome's opponent in the Third Macedonian War. Mention of him is not entirely appropriate since the Roman fleet effected little against him until, having won their land victory at Pydna, the Romans under Cn. Octavius received the surrender of his fleet at Samothrace without striking a blow.

l. 15. **omnibusque navalibus pugnis**: Rhetorical exaggeration. The Romans were defeated in naval battles at Drepana and Cape Pachynus.

l. 16. **Carthaginienses**: During the First Punic War, 264–241.

l. 17. **exercitatissimos paratissimosque**: ' extremely experienced and well equipped '.

l. 20. **salvos praestare**: ' to guarantee our allies' safety '.

l. 21. **Delos**: Well situated to act as an entrepôt for trade between East and West, it flourished greatly after being made a free port in 166 and after the destruction of Corinth by Rome in 146. It was subsequently sacked by Mithridates in 88, and in 69 by the pirates who enslaved the inhabitants, in spite of the fact that it was a large slave market and therefore one of their best customers.

l. 23. **commeabant**: ' used to come together '.

l. 26. **Appia . . . via**: The Appian Way was begun by Appius Claudius the Censor in 312 and runs from Rome to Capua whence it crosses Italy to Brundisium. The first part is within easy reach of the sea.

l. 26. **carebamus**: ' were deprived of the use of ', ' were kept away from '.

l. 28. **cum**: ' although '.

l. 29. **exuviis**: The beaks of the ships captured from Antium. See note on 1, **locus**, p. 34.

Sections 56–58

XIX. 56. line 1. **Bono ... animo**: Here ' with good intentions ', not the more usual ' courageously '.

l. 3. **in salute communi**: ' in a matter concerning the safety of all '.

l. 4. **dolori**: ' distress '.

l. 5. **obtemperare**: ' to pay attention to '.

l. 7. **aliquando**: ' at length '.

57. line 9. **Quo**: ' And therefore '.

l. 10. **obtrectatum esse**: Impersonal. Possibly translate by means of an abstract noun ' the opposition '. It is to be taken both with the datives **Gabinio** etc. and with **ne legaretur**. ' And I therefore think that the opposition previously offered to Gabinius ... in preventing Pompey's earnest requests for his appointment as *legatus* even more intolerable '.

Roman provincial governors and generals were authorized by the Senate to choose the *legati* to serve on their staff. In exceptional cases this authorization was specifically granted by law, and the *lex Gabinia* accorded this right to Pompey. But the *lex Licinia et Aebutia de magistratibus extraordinariis* of the middle of the second century forbade any man who proposed a law to enjoy any office created by that law. This debarred Gabinius from serving as Pompey's *legatus* so long as Pompey derived his *imperium* from the *lex Gabinia*. The *lex Manilia* has of course not yet been passed. The Senate had possibly been asked to grant a *privilegium* or exemption from the laws in Gabinius's case, and had refused. We know that this year more stringent control of the practice of granting *privilegia* was introduced by the *lex Cornelia de privilegiis* of the tribune, C.

Cornelius. The problem was finally solved when Pompey was able to make him a *legatus* after the *lex Manilia* had been passed.

l. 14. **qui impetret**: ' to have his request granted '.

l. 14. **cum**: Concessive.

l. 18. **expers**: Distinguish between **expers** (**ex** and **pars** = having no part in) and **expertus**.

l. 19. **periculo**: ' at his peril ', because he is responsible for the results of his law.

58. line 20. **An**: Take with **sunt tam diligentes**. **C. Falcidius ... potuerunt** and **in uno deberet** are co-ordinate. We should make the first clause subordinate, using a conjunction such as ' while ', because it is only introduced for the sake of the contrast. Cicero is not complaining of the appointment of C. Falcidius and the others, but is asking whether the Senate is not making an exception to its normal practice in its refusal to permit the appointment of Gabinius. This figure of speech, found in both Greek and Latin is known as *parataxis*.

l. 21. **honoris causa**: The regular formula when living men of rank are named, particularly if any disparagement could be read into the mention of them.

l. 23. **diligentes**: ' punctilious ', ' precise '. We have no evidence upon which to base any comparison of the case of Gabinius with that of the other four. We do not know whether they should have been disqualified from being *legati* under the provisions of the *lex Licinia et Aebutia* or whether, as is more likely, they were not responsible during their tribunate for the legislation under which the commander or governor whom they served as *legati* enjoyed his *imperium*.

l. 24. **in hoc imperatore atque exercitu**: The use of the preposition *in* is extended from **in hoc bello** and **in hoc exercitu** to **in hoc imperatore**, although *cum* or *sub* would be more natural.

l. 26. **praecipuo iure esse**: ' to enjoy special privileges '.

l. 27. **ad senatum relaturos**: *refero ad senatum de aliqua re* = I initiate a debate in the Senate.

l. 28. **ego me profiteor relaturum**: Cicero as praetor had this right, but any equal or superior magistrate could veto the introduction of the motion, and the consuls could issue a decree (*edictum*) that no business appearing on the order of the day be introduced.

l. 30. **vestrum ius beneficiumque:** The right granted to Pompey by the *lex Gabinia* of choosing his own *legati*.

l. 31. **intercessionem:** ' tribunician veto '.

l. 32. **quid liceat:** ' how far they may go '. In theory a tribune could veto any motion, but the turbulent political life of Rome since the time of the Gracchi would have taught tribunes — Gabinius's opponent, Trebellius, for example — that their *sacrosanctitas* was no longer the protection that it had once been, and that they had to heed the extent to which public opinion was behind them.

l. 35. **socius ascribitur:** ' is associated with '

Section 59

XX. 59. line 3. **si quid eo factum esset:** ' if anything should happen to him '. **fio** in this sense is used with the dative, the ablative, or ablative and *de*. **factum esset** represents the **factum erit** of direct speech.

l. 5. **magnum ... fructum:** ' a big tribute to '.

l. 5. **cum ... dixistis:** Another example of a past indicative in a *cum*-clause identifying the time at which the action of the main verb took place by giving another action of which it is an equivalent. Here placing hope in Pompey is the equivalent of paying tribute to his qualities.

Section 60

60. line 1. **At enim:** Again introducing the argument of the opposition. A quotation of their words follows.

l. 1. **novi:** Partitive genitive.

l. 2. **Non dicam:** cf. 48, **Non sum praedicaturus,** p. 22, for another example of *praeteritio*.

l. 3. **consuetudini, ... utilitati:** ' precedent, ... expediency '.

l. 4. **novos casus temporum:** ' new emergencies '.

l. 6. **Hispaniense:** Here the Numantine War, elsewhere in this speech the Sertorian.

l. 6. **ab uno imperatore**: Publius Cornelius Scipio Aemilianus destroyed Carthage in 146 and Numantia in 133. His consulship of 147 was illegal because he was below the legal age for that office and had not held the requisite lesser magistracies as set out by the *lex Villia annalis* of 180. That of 134 was also illegal because it transgressed the law of 151 which forbade a second election to the consulship. See Introduction, p. xxxv.

l. 10. **nuper**: Forty years earlier.

l. 10. **esse visum**: ' decided '.

l. 11. **C. Mario**: Marius was consul seven times — in 107, 104–100, and 86. In his first consulship he was in command of the war against Jugurtha whom he finally defeated while proconsul in 105. In 102, during his fourth consulship, he defeated the Teutoni at Aquae Sextiae, and the Cimbri at Vercellae in the following year.

l. 14. **novi . . . nihil**: ' no new precedent '.

Sections 61–63

XXI. 61. For Pompey's early career, see Introduction, pp. xxxix f.

l. 1. **adulescentulum privatum**: These words should be taken together. **privatum**: Not holding public office.

l. 2. **exercitum . . . conficere?**: ' to raise an army '.

l. 5. **a senatorio gradu**: Under the Sullan reorganisation of the Senate, the quaestorship led to automatic membership. Nobody was to be elected quaestor below the age of thirty, yet Pompey was only twenty-four when sent to Sicily.

l. 9. **innocentia**: ' integrity '. Cf. this use in 36, p. 17.

l. 9. **gravitate**: ' dignity '.

l. 9. **virtute**: ' ability '.

l. 10. **deportavit**: The technical term for bringing anything home from the provinces.

l. 11. **equitem Romanum**: The sons of senators who were not yet themselves senators held Equestrian rank.

l. 13. **omnium . . . studio**: ' with universal enthusiasm '.

l. 14. **visendam et concelebrandam**: For the gerundive used predicatively in agreement with the object of a verb, see 7 **denotavit**, p. 42.

62. line 15. **duo consules**: The consuls of 77, Mam. Aemilius Lepidus and D. Junius Brutus.

l. 19. **hominem privatum pro consule**: Proconsular *imperium* could exceptionally be granted to a *privatus*.

l. 20. **L. Philippus**: Consul in 91 and censor in 86, he was the most senior man of consular rank in active politics.

l. 20. **non ... pro consule, sed pro consulibus**: Philippus's word play is used by Cicero as further praise for Pompey.

l. 23. **munus**: ' function '.

l. 25. **ex senatus consulto**: The Senate was competent to grant a *privilegium* or exemption from the provisions of a law.

l. 25. **legibus solutus**: The *lex Villia annalis* of 180 as amended by the *lex Cornelia annalis* of 81 stated that a man must not hold the consulship at an age of less than forty-two nor without having previously been quaestor and praetor.

l. 26. **ullum alium magistratum**: Pompey would be thirty-six, but a man could be elected quaestor at the age of thirty. Cicero cannot be including the quaestorship.

l. 27. **iterum ... triumpharet?**: To enable him to triumph, the Sertorian War had to be considered a war against foreigners, not a civil war.

l. 29. **Quae ...**: ' Not all those departures from precedent which have been made in the cases of individual men since the beginning of history are as numerous as these ...'. **hominibus ... hominum ... homine**: Another example of *traductio*. Cf. 1, **tempus ... temporibus**, p. 1.

l. 31. **in hoc uno homine**: The very reason why the *imperium* should not be given to Pompey. Cicero does not mention the optimate opposition to the *lex Gabinia* in order to be able to make his point in the next sentence.

63. line 31. **Atque haec tot ... tam nova**: The demonstrative adjectives and adverb **tot ... tanta ... tam** will disappear in English.

l. 33. **a Q. Catuli . . . auctoritate.** This overlooks the fact that Pompey's first triumph — *ex Africa* — was granted by Sulla. **amplissimorum hominum** are the *principes* or senatorial leaders.

Sections 63–64

XXII. line 2. **illorum auctoritatem:** No sooner had Sulla set constitutional power in the Senate's hands than that body by a series of measures, such as Pompey's Spanish command, infringed the provisions of the Sullan constitution and helped to destroy his work. Cicero now claims for the people the right to do what the Senate has already done. See Introduction, p. xl.

This sentence contains another example of *parataxis*. See 58, **An**, p. 26.

l. 5. **suo iure:** ' in its own right ', because of the success of the popular legislation in the case of the war against the pirates.

l. 6. **vel:** ' even '.

l. 8. **isdem istis reclamantibus:** ' in spite of the outcry of those same men '.

64. line 10. **consuluistis:** Note case of **rei publicae,** and hence meaning of the verb.

l. 11. **studia:** ' sympathies '.

l. 12. **vidistis:** Here of political insight.

l. 13. **istis repugnantibus:** ' in the face of their opposition '.

l. 14. **aliquando:** ' at last '.

l. 15. **principes:** See previous section.

l. 15. **sibi:** The usual construction, rather than *a* with the ablative, when there is no ambiguity.

Sections 64–68

l. 4. **Difficile est . . . :** The ease with which the riches of the eastern provinces corrupted Roman governors was notorious.

l. 4. **Asia:** The Roman province of Asia, the western portion of the modern Turkey.

l. 5. **interiorum nationum:** ' the peoples of the interior '.

l. 5. **nostrum:** ' sent by us '.

l. 6. **nihil aliud nisi de hoste**: Note the change of construction from the internal accusative to *de* with the ablative. In classical prose the internal accusative is only found with pronouns such as *id, hoc, illud, quid*, and *nihil*.

65. line 12. **libidines**: ' wanton conduct '.

l. 14. **religiosum**: ' sacred '.

l. 16. **copiosae**: Having much **copia**.

l. 16. **quibus . . . inferatur**: ' against whom some pretext for war can be brought to satisfy their greed for plunder '.

66. líne 18. **coram**: ' face to face '.

l. 19. **disputarem**: ' discuss ', not ' dispute '.

l. 22. **hostium simulatione**: ' pretending to attack an enemy '.

l. 22. **socios atque amicos**: See note on 4, **sociis**, p. 37.

l. 23. **Quae civitas . . .**: A Roman governor was attended by a retinue, the size of which was determined by his rank, and the support of which was the responsibility of the provincials.

l. 24. **animos ac spiritus**: ' arrogance and insolence '.

l. 25. **capere**: ' contain '.

XXIII. line 26. **collatis signis**: ' in a pitched battle '.

l. 31. **ad bellum Asiaticum regiumque**: ' a war against an Asiatic monarch '.

67. line 32. **Ecquam**: Another example of *commutatio*. See 31, **ab omnibus . . . imperatore**, p. 15. This sentence means that in Roman eyes a state which was still wealthy had not been pacified, and any that had been pacified would no longer be rich.

l. 34. **istis**: Has the meaning, common in oratory, of ' opponents '.

l. 34. **Ora maritima**: The countries bordering the Mediterranean and liable to pirate attacks.

l. 38. **praetor paucos**: Servilius, mentioned in the next section, who fought the pirates from 78 to 74, is a good example of an honest man. With the word **paucos** Cicero may be doing less than justice to his fellow-countrymen. He is in this speech concerned to show the superior integrity of Pompey, and our own view of Roman conduct in the provinces is inevitably coloured by the fact that much of our primary evidence is drawn from speeches prosecuting the least satisfactory of Roman governors and generals. For each of these rogues there would have been many honest and hard-working officials.

l. 39. **classium nomine:** 'our paper fleets', because the money which should have been spent on them had been embezzled.

l. 39. **maiore:** i.e. than if we had not attempted to raise a fleet.

l. 41. **iacturis:** 'expenditure', i.e. on bribes.

l. 41. **condicionibus:** 'arrangements' to ensure that they could line their own pockets without fear of retribution.

l. 42. **videlicet:** Makes **ignorant** ironical.

l. 43. **omnia:** 'the supreme command'.

l. 43. **quasi vero:** A common ironic introduction in Cicero; 'just as if'.

68. line 46. **qui inter tot annos unus:** 'who for so many years has been the only general'.

Section 68

l. 2. **est vobis auctor vir:** 'you have the authority of a man who'. Cf. note on 1, **huius auctoritatem loci,** p. 35.

l. 3. **P. Servilius:** P. Servilius Vatia Isauricus, consul in 79, proconsul in Asia from 78 to 74, waged a successful war against the pirates from which he received his *agnomen*. Isauria contained the pirates' mountain strongholds in the hinterland of Pamphylia; see map, pp. viii and ix.

l. 6. **C. Curio:** C. Scribonius Curio, consul in 76, proconsul of Macedonia from 75 to 72, whence he returned to Rome to celebrate a triumph over the Dardani.

l. 8. **Cn. Lentulus:** Cn. Cornelius Lentulus Clodianus, consul in 72, censor in 70, a *legatus* of Pompey in the pirate war.

l. 9. **pro . . . honoribus:** 'as became the offices you showered upon him'.

l. 10. **gravitatem:** because of his severity as censor when he expelled sixty-four men from the Senate.

l. 10. **C. Cassius**: C. Cassius Longinus, consul in 73. We have no evidence with which to judge the truth of what Cicero says about him.

l. 12. **auctoritatibus**: ' views ', ' arguments '.

Sections 69–71

XXIV. 69. line 2. **voluntatem et sententiam**: ' your intentions and your proposal '.

l. 4. **auctore**: ' with the support of '.

l. 5. **vim aut minas**: No rhetorical exaggeration. Gabinius had in the previous year been threatened by the Senate, and their *sacrosanctitas* no longer protected tribunes from violence.

l. 8. **iterum**: The first occasion had been to pass the *lex Gabinia*.

l. 9. **de re**: ' concerning the proposal itself '.

70. line 16. **huic loco temploque**: ' this consecrated spot ', i.e. the Rostra. All popular assemblies at Rome had to meet on ground which had been duly consecrated by the augurs.

l. 20. **putem**: The subjunctive implies that the idea is in the mind of others.

l. 22. **quaeram**: A final subjunctive.

l. 23. **praestare**: ' guarantee ', i.e. it is in the hands of the gods.

l. 24. **ex hoc loco**: ' from the Rostra '. Cicero means that advancement will come to him through his work in the law-courts.

71. line 27. **mihi susceptum est**: The meaning of this clause is clear; ' whatever burden I have undertaken in this case '. **mihi** may either be a dative of the agent or, more probably, an extension to the passive of the use with *suscipio* of the dative of the reflexive pronoun. *Suscipio aliquid mihi* =' I take some task upon myself ', ' I undertake some task '.

l. 31. **vobis non inutiles**: See note on 20, *L. Lucullo* p. 55 for the care with which Cicero tried to avoid giving offence to the optimates who opposed the measure he was supporting.

l. 32. **hoc honore**: The urban praetorship.

l. 36. **rationibus**: ' interests '.

BIBLIOGRAPHICAL NOTE

IN addition to this speech which is the main contemporary literary source for the conflict between Rome and Mithridates, there are a number of later writers upon whom we rely for our knowledge of Rome's wars with him and the kingdom of Pontus.

Strabo, a native of Pontus, wrote in Greek a *Geography* in seventeen books which deals extensively with its topography. The text and translation are most conveniently accessible in *The Loeb Classical Library*. Appian of Alexandria, who lived in the second century of our era, wrote in Greek a history of the wars of Rome, one book of which is devoted to the Mithridatic Wars. This text too has been published with a translation in *The Loeb Classical Library*, as have Plutarch's Lives of Sulla, Lucullus, and Pompey, which all deal incidentally with the struggle with Mithridates.

There are many other Greek and Roman writers who cover this period and the most important sources are collected in Greenidge and Clay's *Sources for Roman History* 133–70 B.C., revised by E. W. Gray. A fuller collection of references with some important analyses of problems (e.g. The date of the outbreak of the Third Mithridatic War) is given in Broughton's *The Magistrates of the Roman Republic*, Vol. II.

Modern works are Th. Reinach's *Mithridate Eupator*; the *Cambridge Ancient History*, Vol. IX, Chs. v and viii; and, most valuable of all, D. Magie, *Roman Rule in Asia Minor*. A biography of Mithridates by Alfred Duggan entitled *He Died Old* is written for the non-specialist reader.

The *Cambridge Ancient History*, Vol. IX, contains a full account of this period but needs bringing up to date. A much shorter account of events is contained in the relevant chapters of H. H. Scullard's *From the Gracchi to Nero*, which has the additional value of references in the notes to more recently published books and articles.

Cicero has not of late been as well served by English scholars as have other Latin authors; and while his text and historical problems of his life have received attention, no full-scale study has appeared in the last twenty years. For his style, D. Broadhead, *Latin Prose Rhythm*, may be consulted, and more general books published since the war are H. A. K. Hunt, *The Humanism of Cicero*, and F. R. Cowell, *Cicero and the Roman Republic*. The first volume of *Studies in Latin Literature and its Influence* is devoted to Cicero and contains a number of assessments of his life and work which show the lines along which modern scholarship is advancing. A number of the chapters contain material useful to the student of this speech.

VOCABULARY

THE perfects and supines of all verbs of the third conjugation and of all irregular verbs are given. Otherwise the figure following a verb denotes that it is a regular example of that conjugation. The omission of a perfect or supine indicates that it is not in normal use.

a, ab, *prep. with abl.,* from, by.
abdo, -didi, -ditum (3), *tr.,* hide.
absens, -ntis, absent, distant.
absum, -esse, afui, *intr.,* am away, am distant; **tantum abest ut,** it is so far from being the case that.
ac, *conj., see* atque.
accido, -di, (3), *intr.,* happen.
accipio, -cepi, -ceptum (3), *tr.,* receive, hear.
accommodo (1), *tr.,* adapt.
accuratissime, *superl. adv.,* very carefully.
acer, acris, acre, active, energetic.
ad, *prep. with acc.,* to, for.
adduco, -xi, -ctum (3), *tr.,* lead.
adeo, -ii, -itum (4), *tr. and intr.,* approach.
adfero, -ferre, attuli, -latum, *tr.,* bring, bring to.
adficio, -feci, -fectum (3), *tr.,* treat, provide with, honour.
adfingo, -nxi, -ctum (3), *tr.,* invent, add falsely.
adfligo, -xi, -ctum (3), *tr.,* throw down.
adhuc, *adv.,* hitherto.
adimo, -emi, -emptum (3), *tr.,* take away.
aditus, -us, *m.,* approach, access.
adiumentum, -i, *n.,* aid, help.

adiungo, -nxi, -nctum (3), *tr.,* join, unite.
adlicio, -lexi, -lectum (3), *tr.,* attract, entice.
administra, -ae, *f.,* handmaid, helper.
administro (1), *tr.,* manage, conduct.
admoneo (2), *tr.,* remind.
admurmuratio, -ionis, *f.,* murmuring.
adorno (1), *tr.,* furnish, equip.
adsentio, -si, -sum (4), *intr. with dat.,* agree with.
adsequor, -secutus sum (3), *tr.,* attain.
adsum, -esse, -fui, *intr.,* am present.
adulescens, -ntis, *m.,* youth.
adulescentia, -ae, *f.,* youth.
adulescentulus, -i, *m.,* very young man.
adventicius, -a, -um, foreign.
adventus, -us, *m.,* arrival.
aedifico (1), *tr.,* build.
aegre, *adv.,* scarcely, with difficulty.
aequus, -a, -um, fair, reasonable.
aerarium, -i, *n.,* treasury.
aestas, -atis, *f.,* summer.
aetas, -atis, *f.,* time of life, age.
ager, agri, *m.,* field, land.

91

agito (1), disturb, excite.

agnosco, -novi, -nitum (3), *tr.*, recognize.

ago, egi, actum (3), *tr.*, drive, do; speak, discuss, plead a case, submit a question; *impers.*, come; *pass. pers. or impers.*, am in question, at stake.

aio, *defect., intr.*, say

alienus, -a, -um, of another.

aliquando, *adv.*, some time, at last.

aliqui, -qua, -quod, *indef. adj.*, some.

aliquis, -quid, *indef. pron.*, some one, some thing.

aliquot, *indecl. adj.*, some.

alius, -a, -ud, other.

alter, -era, -erum, one of two, the other, second.

amicus, -a, -um, friendly.

amicus, -i, *m.*, a friend.

amitto, -misi, -missum (3), *tr.*, lose.

amo (1), *tr.*, love; **amans, -ntis,** *with gen.*, devoted to.

amoenitas, -atis, *f.*, beauty.

amplifico (1), *tr.*, increase, enlarge.

amplitudo, -inis, *f.*, greatness, honour.

amplus, -a, -um, large, spacious, splendid, honourable.

an, *conj.*, or, *after* utrum *or* -ne; *also used elliptically to ask single questions.*

anceps, -ipitis, double, on two fronts.

animus, -i, *m.*, mind, intention, spirit, courage; *in. pl.*, pride.

anne, *see* an.

annus, -i, *m.*, year.

ante, *adv.*, before; *prep. with*

acc., before; **ante quam,** *conj.*, before.

antea, *adv.*, before.

antecello (3), *defect., intr. with dat.*, surpass.

antiquitas, -atis, *f.*, former times, those living in former times.

aperio, -ui, -tum (4), *tr.*, open.

apertus, -a, -um, undisguised.

apparo (1), *tr.*, prepare.

appello (1), *tr.*, address.

appeto, -ivi, -itum (3), *tr.*, strive after; **appetens, -ntis,** *with gen.*, eager for.

apud, *prep. with acc.*, among, with.

arbitror (1), *tr.*, consider.

argentum, -i, *n.*, silver.

arma, -orum, *n. plur.*, arms.

ars, artis, *f.*, art, skill, quality.

ascribo, -psi, -ptum (3), *tr.*, join to, include among, enrol.

assiduitas, -atis, *f.*, perseverance.

at, *conj.*, but; **at enim,** but surely, but it will be said.

atque, *conj.*, and, and in addition.

attenuo (1), *tr.*, weaken.

attingo, -tigi, -tactum (3), *tr.*, touch, reach.

auctor, -oris, *m.*, leader, supporter.

auctoritas, -atis, *f.*, authority, judgement, influence, prestige.

audeo, ausus sum (2), *tr. and intr.*, dare.

audio (4), *tr.*, hear.

aufero, auferre, abstuli, ablatum, *tr.*, carry off.

auris, -is, *f.*, ear.

aurum, -i, *n.*, gold.

aut, *conj.*, or; **aut . . . aut,** either . . . or.

autem, *conj.*, but, moreover.

auxilium, -i, *n.*, help; *plur.*, auxiliary troops.

avaritia, -ae, *f.*, greed.

avidus, -a, -um, greedy for.

avitus, -a, -um, of a grandfather, ancestral.

barbarus, -a, -um, foreign, barbarous.

beatus, -a, -um, happy, fortunate.

bello (1), *intr.*, carry on war.

bellum, -i, *n.*, war.

beneficium, -i, *n.*, favour, kindness.

bini, -ae, -a, two each.

bonus, -a, -um, good; bona, -orum, *n. plur.*, property.

brevis, -e, short.

breviter, *adv.*, shortly.

caelum, -i, *n.*, heaven.

calamitas, -atis, *f.*, disaster.

capio, cepi, captum (3), *tr.*, take, capture, hold, contain.

careo (2), *intr. with abl.*, lack, want, am deprived of.

caritas, -atis, *f.*, dearness, high price.

caste, *adv.*, uprightly, conscientiously.

casus, -us, *m.*, chance, event.

causa, -ae, *f.*, cause, reason, case; *abl. used with gen.*, for the sake of.

celeber, -bris, -bre, crowded.

celeritas, -atis, *f.*, speed.

celeriter, *adv.*, quickly.

centuria, -ae, *f.*, century.

centuriatus, -us, *m.*, rank of centurion.

certus, -a, -um, fixed, certain,

definite; certe, *adv.*, surely, certainly.

ceterus, -a, -um, the rest, the remainder.

cingo, cinxi, cinctum (3), *tr.*, surround.

civilis, -e, civil.

civis, -is, *c.*, citizen.

civitas, -atis, *f.*, state.

clarus, -a, -um, famous, illustrious, glorious.

classis, -is, *f.*, fleet.

claudo, clausi, clausum (3), *tr.*, shut.

coepi, coepisse, *defect.*, *intr.*, begin; coeptus sum *when followed by pass. inf.*

cogito (1), *tr.*, think.

cognitio, -onis, *f.*, learning, making acquaintance.

cognosco, -novi, -nitum (3), *tr.*, learn; *perf.*, know.

cogo, coegi, coactum (3), *tr.*, compel.

cohaereo, -si, -sum (2), *intr.*, cling to.

cohibeo (2), *tr.*, keep back, restrain.

collectio, -onis, *f.*, collection.

colligo, -legi, -lectum (3), *tr.*, collect.

colloco (1), *tr.*, place, invest (*money*).

comes, -itis, *c.*, companion.

comitia, -orum, *n. plur.*, assembly, election.

commeatus, -us, *m.*, movement to and fro, communication.

commemoro (1), *tr.*, mention.

commendo (1), *tr.*, entrust.

commeo (1), *intr.*, resort to.

committo, -misi, -missum (3), *tr.*, entrust.

commodum, -i, *n.,* interest.
commoror (1), *intr.,* stay.
commoveo, -movi, -motum (2), *tr.,* influence.
commune, -is, *n.,* community, diet.
communis, -e, common, general.
comparatio, -onis, *f.,* preparation.
comparo (1), *tr.,* prepare.
compleo, -evi, -etum (2), *tr.,* fill.
complures, -a, several, very many.
comprobo (1), *tr.,* approve.
concedo, -cessi, -cessum (3), *tr. and intr.,* yield, retire, allow.
concelebro (1), *tr.,* crowd, celebrate in great numbers.
concerto (1), *intr.,* dispute.
concido, -cidi (3), *intr.,* fall, fail.
concilio (1), *tr.,* win, win over.
concipio, -cepi, -ceptum (3), *tr.,* receive, incur.
concito (1), *tr.,* stir up.
concupisco, -pivi, -pitum (3), *tr.,* covet.
conditio, -onis, *f.,* terms, agreement.
confero, -ferre, -tuli, -latum, *tr.,* bring together, apply, devote; *with reflex. pron.,* withdraw.
conficio, -feci, -fectum, *tr.,* finish, complete, procure, provide.
confirmo (1), *tr.,* strengthen, encourage, assert.
confiteor, -fessus sum (2), *tr. and intr.,* confess.
confligo, -xi, -ctum (3), *intr.,* struggle with, fight.
congero, -gessi, -gestum (3), *tr.,* bring together, collect.
coniectura, -ae, *f.,* inference.

coniungo, -iunxi, -iunctum (3), *tr.,* join, act in concert.
coniunx, -iugis, *f.,* wife.
conor (1), *intr.,* try.
conquiesco, -evi, -etum (3), *intr.,* rest, am inactive.
consequor, -secutus sum (3), *tr. and intr.,* follow, reach, obtain.
conservo (1), *tr.,* keep safe.
considero (1), *tr.,* consider, examine.
consilium, -i, *n.,* plan, policy, judgement, foresight, prudence.
conspectus, -us, *m.,* sight, appearance.
conspicio, -spexi, -spectum (3), *tr.,* see, view.
constantia, -ae, *f.,* firmness.
constituo, -ui, -utum (3), *tr.,* appoint, decide, determine, establish, constitute.
consuetudo, -inis, *f.,* custom, precedent.
consul, -ulis, *m.,* consul.
consularis, -is, *m.,* man of consular rank, ex-consul.
consulo, -ui, -tum (3), *tr.,* consult; *intr. with dat.,* have regard for.
consulto, *adv.,* purposely.
consultum, -i, *n.,* decree.
contemno, -tempsi, -temptum (3), *tr.,* despise, spurn.
contendo, -di, -tum (3), *intr.,* fight.
contentio, -onis, *f.,* struggle; comparison.
contentus, -a, -um, content.
continentia, -ae, *f.,* self-restraint.
contineo, -tinui, -tentum (2), *tr.,* check, restrain.

continuus, -a, -um, uninterrupted, successive.

contra, *prep. with acc.,* against.

contrarius, -a, -um, opposing, conflicting.

convenio, -veni, -ventum (4), *intr.,* come together, meet; *impers.,* it is fitting, proper.

copia, -ae, *f.,* plenty, ability, fluency; *plur.,* resources, wealth; forces, troops.

copiosus, -a, -um, rich, well-supplied.

coram, *adv.,* face to face.

cotidianus, -a, -um, daily.

cotidie, *adv.,* daily.

credo, -idi, -itum (3), *tr.,* entrust; *intr. with dat.,* believe.

cresco, crevi, cretum (3), *intr.,* increase, grow.

culpa, -ae, *f.,* fault.

cultura, -ae, *f.,* cultivation.

cum, *conj.,* when, since; **cum . . . tum,** both . . . and.

cum, *prep. with abl.,* with.

cunctus, -a, -um, all, the whole.

cupiditas, -atis, *f.,* desire, eagerness, greed.

cupidus, -a, -um, greedy, avaricious.

cupio, -ivi, -itum (3), *tr.,* desire, wish.

cur, *adv.,* why.

cura, -ae, *f.,* care, trouble, anxiety: **curae esse,** to be an object of care.

curo (1), *tr.,* see to, order.

cursus, -us, *m.,* journey, voyage.

custodia, -ae, *f.,* guard, guardpost.

de, *prep. with abl.,* about, concerning.

debeo (2), *tr. and intr.,* owe, am bound to, ought.

declaro (1), *tr.,* declare, prove.

decuma, -ae, *f.,* tenth part, tithe.

deditio, -onis, *f.,* surrender.

dedo, -didi, -ditum (3), *tr.,* give up, surrender.

defendo, -di, -sum (3), *tr.,* defend.

defero, -ferre, -tuli, -latum, *tr.,* carry down, deliver, grant, confer; announce, report.

deinde, *adv.,* next.

delabor, -lapsus sum (3), *intr.,* descend.

delectatio, -onis, *f.,* delight, enjoyment.

deleo, -evi, -etum (2), *tr.,* destroy.

deliberatio, -onis, *f.,* consideration.

delibero (1), *intr.,* deliberate.

deligo, -legi, -lectum (3), *tr.,* choose.

denique, *adv.,* finally, in short.

depello, -puli, -pulsum (3), *tr.,* drive away, drive off.

deporto (1), *tr.,* carry away, bring home.

deposco, -poposci (3), *tr.,* demand.

deprecator, -oris, *m.,* suppliant.

deprimo, -pressi, -pressum (3), *tr.,* sink.

depromo, -mpsi, -mptum (3), *tr.,* draw out, draw.

desero, -ui, -tum (3), *tr.,* desert.

desertus, -a, -um, desert.

desiderium, -i, *n.,* longing.

desum, -esse, -fui, *intr. with dat.,* am lacking, fail.

detraho, -traxi, -tractum (3), *tr.,* take away, remove.

detrimentum, -i, *n.,* loss.

deus, -i, *m.,* god.

devoco (1), *tr.,* call away, entice.

dico, dixi, dictum (3), *tr.*, say, speak.

dies, -ei, *c.*, day.

differo, differre, distuli, dilatum, *intr.*, differ.

difficilis, -e, difficult.

diffido, -fisus sum (3), *intr. with dat.*, distrust.

dignitas, -atis, *f.*, merit, desert, rank, greatness.

dignus, -a, -um, worthy.

dilatio, -onis, *f.*, postponement.

diligens, -ntis, careful, particular.

diligenter, *adv.*, carefully.

diligo, -lexi, -lectum (3), *tr.*, love.

dimico (1), *intr.*, fight.

dimitto, -misi, -missum (3), *tr.*, send away, discharge.

diripio, -ripui, -reptum (3), *tr.*, seize, plunder.

discedo, -cessi, -cessum (3), *intr.*, go away, depart, withdraw.

disciplina, -ae, *f.*, training, instruction.

discrimen, -inis, *n.*, risk, danger, crisis.

disiunctus, -a, -um, distant, remote.

disiungo, -nxi, -nctum (3), *tr.*, divide.

dispergo, -si, -sum (3), *tr.*, scatter.

disputo (1), *tr.*, discuss.

dissentio, -si, -sum (4), *intr.*, disagree.

dissipo (1), *tr.*, scatter.

distringo, -nxi, -ctum (3), *tr.*, divide, occupy.

diu, *adv.*, for a long time; *comp.*, diutius; *superl.*, diutissime.

diuturnitas, -atis, *f.*, length, long duration.

diuturnus, -a, -um, long.

diversus, -a, -um, distant, different.

divido, -si, -sum (3), *tr.*, divide, separate.

divinitus, *adv.*, by divine intervention.

divinus, -a, -um, divine.

divitiae, -arum, *f.*, *plur.*, wealth.

do, dedi, datum (1), *tr.*, give.

doceo (2), *tr.*, teach.

dolor, -oris, *m.*, grief.

domicilium, -i, *n.*, dwelling, home.

domus, -us, *f.*, home; *loc.*, domi, at home.

dubito (1), *intr.*, doubt, hesitate.

dubius, -a, -um, doubtful.

duco, duxi, ductum (3), *tr.*, lead, think.

ductus, -us, *m.*, lead, leadership, conduct.

dum, *conj.*, while, until, provided that.

duo, -ae, -o, two.

duodecim, *indecl. adj.*, twelve.

dux, ducis, *c.*, leader.

e, ex, *prep. with abl.*, from, out of, in accordance with.

ecqui, ecquae *or* ecqua, ecquod, *interrog. adj.*, any?

educo, -duxi, -ductum (3), *tr.*, lead out.

efficio, -feci, -fectum (3), *tr.*, achieve, bring about.

effugio, -fugi (3), *intr.*, escape.

ego, mei, I.

egregius, -a, -um, outstanding, exceptional.

elaboro (1), *tr.*, work out, elaborate.

emergo, -si, -sum (3), *intr.*, arise.

enim, *conj.*, for.

eques, -itis, *m.*, horseman; member of the Equestrian Order.

equitatus, -us, *m.*, cavalry.

erigo, -rexi, -rectum (3), *tr.*, raise.

eripio, -ripui, -reptum (3), *tr.*, take, snatch away.

erudio (4), *tr.*, train, instruct.

escendo, -di, -sum (3), *tr.*, go up, climb.

et, *conj.*, and; **et . . . et,** both . . . and.

etenim, *conj.*, and indeed.

etiam, *adv. and conj.*, even, also; **etiam atque etiam,** again and again.

ex, *see* **e.**

excello, -ui (3), *intr. with dat.*, excel, surpass.

excipio, -cepi, -ceptum (3), *tr.*, take, receive.

excito (1), *tr.*, arouse.

excrucio (1), *tr.*, torture.

excursio, -onis, *f.*, raid.

exemplum, -i, *n.*, example, precedent.

exerceo (2), *tr.*, exercise, employ, practise, conduct.

exercitatio, -onis, *f.*, exercise, practice.

exercito (1), *tr.*, practise, train.

exercitus, -us, *m.*, army.

exigo, -egi, -actum (3), *tr.*, exact.

eximius, -a, -um, extraordinary, outstanding, distinguished.

existimo (1), *tr.*, think.

exitus, -us, *m.*, end.

exorsus, -us, *m.*, beginning.

expello, -puli, -pulsum (3), *tr.*, drive out, expel, banish.

expers, -tis, *with gen.*, without part in.

expeto, -ivi, -itum (3), *tr.*, seek, desire, beg.

expilo (1), *tr.*, plunder.

explico, -avi *or* **-ui, -atum** *or* **-itum** (1), *tr.*, unfold, disentangle, extricate.

exploro (1), *tr.*, explore.

exporto (1), *tr.*, export.

expugnatio, -onis, *f.*, taking by assault, capture.

exquiro, -sivi, -situm (3), *tr.*, search out, discover.

exsisto, -stiti, -stitum (3), *intr.*, emerge, appear, exist.

exspectatio, -onis, *f.*, awaiting, expectation.

exspecto (1), *tr.*, await.

exstinguo, -nxi, -nctum (3), *tr.*, put out, destroy.

exterus, -a, -um, foreign.

extremus, -a, -um, furthest, last, utmost.

exuro, -ussi, -ustum (3), *tr.*, burn.

exuviae, -arum, *f. plur.*, spoils.

facile, *adv.*, easily.

facilis, -e, easy.

facilitas, -atis, *f.*, ease of manner, affability, courteousness.

facio, feci, factum (3), *tr.*, do, make.

facultas, -atis, *f.*, ability, capacity, opportunity.

falso, *adv.*, falsely.

falsus, -a, -um, false, untrue.

fama, -ae, *f.*, report, rumour, reputation.

familia, -ae, *f.*, household (*including slaves*), establishment.

fanum, -i, *n.*, temple.

fateor, fassus sum (2), *tr. and intr.*, admit, acknowledge.

felicitas, -atis, *f.*, good fortune.

fere, *adv.*, nearly, generally.

fero, ferre, tuli, latum, *tr. and
intr.*, carry, bear, endure; require, demand, allow.
fertilis, -e, fertile.
fides, -ei, *f.*, faith, trust, confidence, credit; good faith,
honesty.
finitimi, -orum, *m. plur.*, neighbours.
finitimus, -a, -um, bordering on,
neighbouring.
fio, fieri, factus sum, *intr.*, am
made, am done, become, happen.
firmamentum, -i, *n.*, support.
firmus, -a, -um, firm, strong.
forensis, -e, of the *forum*, connected with trials.
formido, -inis, *f.*, fear.
formidolosus, -a, -um, dreadful,
dangerous.
fors, fortis, *f.*, chance.
fortasse, *adv.*, perhaps.
forte (*abl. of fors*), by chance.
fortis, -e, strong, brave.
fortitudo, -inis, *f.*, bravery.
fortuna, -ae, *f.*, luck, fortune.
forum, -i, *n.*, market-place,
forum (particularly the meet-
ing-place for business at
Rome).
frater, -tris, *m.*, brother.
frequens, -ntis, crowded.
fretus, -a, -um, relying on.
fructus, -us, *m.*, enjoyment, pro-
duce, profit, reward.
frumentarius, -a, -um, of grain,
of provisions; **frumentaria
subsidia**, sources of corn
supply, granaries; **res frumentaria**, provisions.
fruor, fructus sum (3). *intr. with
abl.*, enjoy.

fuga, -ae, *f.*, flight.
fugio, fugi (3), *tr. and intr.*, flee,
escape.

gaudeo, gavisus sum (2), *intr.*,
rejoice.
gaza, -ae, *f.*, treasure.
gens, gentis, *f.*, clan, race, people.
genus, -eris, *n.*, kind, class,
nature, character.
gero, gessi, gestum (3), *tr.*, carry
on, do.
gloria, -ae, *f.*, glory, fame.
gnavus, -a, -um, busy, energetic.
gradus, -us, *m.*, step, degree,
rank.
gratia, -ae, *f.*, favour.
gravis, -e, heavy, serious, important; oppressive; dignified.
gravitas, -atis, *f.*, weight, dignity.
graviter, *adv.*, with weight, with
dignity.
gravor (1), *intr.*, hesitate, am
reluctant.
guberno (1), *tr. and intr.*, steer,
navigate.

habeo (2), *tr.*, have, hold.
hercules, *interj.*, by Hercules.
hiberna, -orum, *n. plur.*, winter
quarters.
hiberno (1), *intr.*, pass the winter,
stay in winter quarters.
hic, haec, hoc, this.
hic, here, now.
hice, haece, hoce, *emphatic form
of* hic.
hiems, -emis, *f.*, winter.
hodie, *adv.*, today.
homo, -inis, *c.*, human being,
man.
honestus, -a, -um, honourable,
distinguished.

honos *and* honor, -oris, *m.*, honour, respect, public office.

hortor (1), *tr.*, exhort.

hostilis, -e, of an enemy, hostile.

hostis, -is, *m.*, enemy.

huc, *adv.*, to this *or* that place, hither.

humanitas, -atis, *f.*, refinement, kindness.

iactura, -ae, *f.*, loss.

iam, *adv.*, now, already.

idem, eadem, idem, same.

idoneus, -a, -um, fit, suitable.

igitur, *conj.*, therefore.

ignominia, -ae, *f.*, disgrace.

ignoro (1), *tr.*, am ignorant of.

ille, illa, illud, that, the well-known, the following.

immineo (2), *intr. with dat.;* *defect.*, threaten.

imminuo, -ui, -utum (3), *tr.*, lessen, violate.

immortalis, -e, immortal.

impedio (4), *tr.*, hinder.

imperator, -oris, *m.*, commander-in-chief.

imperatorius, -a, -um, of a commander-in-chief.

imperium, -i, *n.*, command, dominion.

impero (1), *intr. with dat.*, command; *tr.*, demand, exact.

impertio (4), *tr.*, share, bestow.

impetro (1), *tr.*, obtain (*by asking*).

impetus, -us, *m.*, attack, force.

implico, -avi *or* -ui, -atum *or* -itum (1), *tr.*, involve.

improbo (1), *tr.*, disapprove, reject.

impudens, -ntis, shameless, arrogant.

in, *prep. with acc.*, into, to, against; *with abl.*, in, on, among.

inauditus, -a, -um, unheard of, new, strange.

incipio, -cepi, -ceptum (3), *intr.*, begin.

incolumis, -e, uninjured, safe.

incommodum, -i, *n.*, trouble, misfortune, disaster.

incredibilis, -e, incredible.

incumbo, -cubui, -cubitum (3), *intr.*, lean on; *with prep.*, ad, apply myself to.

inde, *adv.*, from there, thence.

indignus, -a, -um, unworthy, shameful.

industria, -ae, *f.*, diligence, industry, care.

industrius, -a, -um, active, energetic.

ineo, -ire, -ii, -itum, *tr. and intr.*, enter, begin.

infero, -ferre, -tuli, -latum, *tr.*, bring to; bellum alicui, make war upon someone.

infimus, -a, -um, lowest.

inflammo (1), *tr.*, kindle, rouse, excite.

inflo (1), *tr.*, breathe into, puff up.

ingenium, -i, *n.*, nature, ability.

ingratus, -a, -um, ungrateful.

inicio, -ieci, -iectum (3), *tr.*, strike into, inspire.

inimicus, -a, -um, hostile.

inimicus, -i, *m.*, enemy.

iniquitas, -atis, *f.*, unfairness.

initium, -i, *n.*, beginning.

iniuria, -ae, *f.*, wrong, injury.

iniuriose, *adv.*, unjustly, insultingly.

innocens, -ntis, blameless, honest.

innocentia, -ae, *f.*, blamelessness, uprightness.

innumerabilis, -e, countless.

inopia, -ae, *f.*, scarcity, want.

inquam, *defect. intr.*, say.

inruptio, -onis, *f.*, inroad, invasion.

insido, -sedi, -sessum (3), *intr.*, settle on, be rooted in, adhere to.

insigne, -is, *n.*, mark, badge, token.

insolitus, -a, -um, unaccustomed, unusual.

inspecto (1), *tr.*, look at, look upon.

instituo, -ui, utum (3), *tr.*, determine, settle, establish.

institutum, -i, *n.*, practice, custom.

instruo, -xi, -ctum (3), *tr.*, draw up, prepare, equip.

insula, -ae, *f.*, island.

insum, -esse, -fui, am in, belong to.

integer, -gra, -grum, whole, unharmed.

integre, *adv.*, honestly.

integritas, -atis, *f.*, integrity, honesty, honour.

intellego, -lexi, -lectum (3), *tr.*, learn, understand.

inter, *prep. with acc.*, among, between, during.

intercessio, -onis, *f.*, veto.

interficio, -feci, -fectum (3), *tr.*, kill.

interior, -us, inner.

internicio, -onis, *f.*, slaughter, massacre.

intra, *prep. with acc.*, within.

intueor (2), *tr.*, look upon, regard.

inultus, -a, -um, unpunished.

inusitatus, -a, -um, unusual.

inutilis, -e, useless.

invenio, -veni, -ventum (4), *tr.*, find, get.

inveterasco, -avi (3), *intr.*, grow old, become fixed *or* established.

invictus, -a, -um, unconquered.

invisus, -a, -um, hated, hateful.

invitus, -a, -um, unwilling.

ipse, -a, -um, oneself, self, in person.

irascor, iratus sum (3), *intr. with dat.*, am angry with.

is, ea, id, that; he, she, it.

iste, ista, istud, that, that of yours.

ita, *adv.*, thus, so, so far.

itaque, *conj.*, and so, accordingly.

item, *adv.*, in the same way, likewise.

iter, itineris, *n.*, journey, march, road.

iterum, *adv.*, a second time, again.

iucundus, -a, -um, pleasant, welcome.

iudex, -icis, *m.*, judge.

iudicium, -i, *n.*, decision, judgement.

iudico (1), *tr.*, judge.

iure, *adv.*, rightly.

ius, iuris, *n.*, right, justice.

iussu (*abl. only*), *m.*, command, order.

iuvo, iuvi, iutum (1), *tr.*, help.

labefacio, -feci, -factum (3), *tr.*, shake down, make fall, overthrow.

labes, -is, *f.*, stain, disgrace, ruin.

labor, -oris, *m.*, work, labour, effort, exertion.

laboriosus, -a, -um, laborious, toilsome.

laboro (1), *intr.*, work, care, exert myself.

lacesso, -ivi, -itum (3), *tr.*, provoke.

laetitia, -ae, *f.*, joy.

laetor (1), *intr.*, *except with neut. pron.*, rejoice, rejoice at.

late, *adv.*, widely.

latebra, -ae, *f.*, hiding-place.

lateo, -ui (2), *intr.*, lie hid, escape notice.

laudo (1), *tr.*, praise.

laus, laudis, *f.*, praise, fame, renown.

legatio, -onis, *f.*, office of ambassador, embassy.

legatus, -i, *m.*, envoy, ambassador, lieutenant.

legio, -onis, *f.*, legion.

lego, legi, lectum (3), *tr.*, read.

lego (1), *tr.*, appoint as lieutenant.

lex, legis, *f.*, law.

libenter, *adv.*, willingly, gladly.

liber, -era, -erum, free.

libere, *adv.*, freely.

liberi, -orum, *m.*, *plur.*, children.

libero (1), *tr.*, free.

libertas, -atis, *f.*, freedom.

libido, -inis, *f.*, desire, self-indulgence, excess, lust.

licet, licuit, licitum est, *impers. intr. with dat.*, it is allowed.

littera, -ae, *f.*, *sing.*, letter (*of the alphabet*); *plur.*, letter, dispatch.

locuples, -etis, rich, wealthy.

locupleto (1), *tr.*, make rich.

locus, -i, *m.*, place.

longe, *adv.*, far off, far.

longinquitas, -atis, *f.*, distance.

longinquus, -a, -um, distant.

longus, -a, -um, long.

loquor, locutus sum (3), *tr. and intr.*, speak.

ludus, -i, *m.*, game, play, school.

lumen, -inis, *n.*, light, glory.

lux, lucis, *f.*, light, aid, help.

macula, -ae, *f.*, stain, blot, disgrace.

maeror, -oris, *m.*, grief.

magis, *comp. adv.*, more.

magistratus, -us, *m.*, civil office, magistracy; official, magistrate.

magnitudo, -inis, *f.*, size, importance.

magnus, -a, -um, great, large, important.

maior, -us, larger, older.

maiores, -um, *m.*, ancestors.

malo, malle, malui, *intr.*, prefer.

malum, -i, *n.*, evil, calamity.

mando (1), *tr.*, entrust.

maneo, mansi, mansum (2), *intr.*, remain.

mansuetudo, -inis, *f.*, gentleness.

manus, -us, *f.*, hand; band of men, company.

mare, -is, *n.*, sea.

maritimus, -a, -um, of the sea, maritime.

maturus, -a, -um, early.

maxime, *adv.*, very, too much, most of all.

maximus, -a, -um, *superl.*, very great, greatest.

medeor (2), *intr. with dat.*, heal, remedy.

medius, -a, -um, mid, in the middle of.

membrum, -i, *n.*, limb.

memini, meminisse, *defect., tr. and intr. with gen.,* remember.

memoria, -ae, *f.,* memory, recollection.

mens, mentis, *f.,* mind, thought.

mercator, -oris, *m.,* merchant.

merx, mercis, *f.,* merchandise.

metuo, -ui (3), *tr.,* fear.

metus, -us, *m.,* fear.

meus, -a, -um, my.

miles, -itis, *m.,* soldier.

militaris, -e, of soldiers, military.

militia, -ae, *f.,* military service, warfare; **militiae,** *loc.,* in the field, on military service.

mille, *indecl. adj.,* thousand; **milia, -um,** *n. plur.,* thousands.

minae, -arum, *f. plur.,* threats.

minitor (1), *intr. with dat.,* threaten.

minus, *comp. adv.,* less.

miror (1), *tr. and intr.,* wonder at, wonder.

misceo, miscui, mixtum (2), *tr.,* mix.

miseria, -ae, *f.,* wretchedness.

misericordia, -ae, *f.,* pity.

mitto, misi, missum (3), *tr.,* send.

moderatio, -onis, *f.,* moderation, restraint.

moderatus, -a, -um, moderate, keeping within bounds, restrained.

modo, *adv.,* only, just now.

modus, -i, *m.,* limit, way, manner; **eius modi,** of that sort.

molestus, -a, -um, annoying, troublesome.

mors, mortis, *f.,* death.

motus, -us, *m.,* movement.

multitudo, -inis, *f.,* crowd, multitude.

multum, *adv.,* much, very; **multo,** by much, much.

multus, -a, -um, much, many.

munio (4), *tr.,* protect.

munus, -eris, *n.,* duty, office.

murus, -i, *m.,* wall.

nam, *conj.,* for.

nascor, natus sum (3), *intr.,* born.

natio, -onis, *f.,* tribe, people.

nauticus, -a, -um, of ships.

navalis, -e, naval.

navicularius, -i, *m.,* ship-owner.

navigatio, -onis, *f.,* sailing.

navigo (1), *intr.,* sail.

navis, -is, *f.,* ship.

ne, *conj.,* that . . . not, lest; **ne** . . . **quidem,** not . . . even.

nec, see **neque.**

necessarius, -a, -um, necessary.

necessitudo, -inis, *f.,* close connexion.

neco (1), *tr.,* kill.

neglego, -xi, -ctum (3), *tr.,* neglect, disregard.

negotior (1), *intr.,* do business.

negotium, -i, *n.,* business, undertaking.

nemo, nullius, *c.,* no one; **non nemo,** some one.

neque *or* **nec,** *conj.,* and not, nor; **neque** . . . **neque,** neither . . . nor; **neque enim,** for . . . not.

nervus, -i, *m.,* sinew.

neve, *conj., after a clause with* **ut** *or* **ne,** and that . . . not, nor.

nihil, *indecl.,* nothing.

nimis, *adv.,* too, too much.

nimius, -a, -um, too great, excessive.

nisi, *conj.,* if . . . not, unless.

nobilis, -e, famous, noble.

nobilitas, -atis, *f.,* fame, renown.

noceo (2), *intr. with dat.*, hurt.
nolo, nolle, nolui, *intr.*, am unwilling.
nomen, -inis, *n.*, name.
nomino (1), *tr.*, name.
non, *adv.*, not.
nondum, *adv.*, not yet.
nosco, novi, notum (3), *tr.*, get to know, learn.
noster, -tra, -trum, our.
novus, -a, -um, new, recent.
nullus, -a, -um, no, none.
num, *interrog. part.*, whether.
numerus, -i, *m.*, number, rank, place, account.
numquam, *adv.*, never.
nunc, *adv.*, now.
nuntius, -i, *m.*, message, messenger.
nuper, *adv.*, lately.

ob, *prep. with acc.*, on account of.
obeo, -ire, -ii, -itum, *tr.*, enter upon, engage in.
obfero, -ferre, -tuli, -latum, *tr.*, offer, present.
oblivio, -onis, *f.*, forgetfulness.
oboedio (4), *intr., with dat.*, obey.
obscurus, -a, -um, dark, obscure.
obsecundo (1), *intr.*, am compliant, show obedience.
obses, -idis, *c.*, hostage.
obsidio, -onis, *f.*, siege.
obsolesco, -evi, -etum (3), *intr.*, fall into disuse, become obsolete.
obtempero (1), *intr. with dat.*, comply with, submit to.
obtrecto (1), *intr. with dat.*, decry, oppose.
occasio, -onis, *f.*, opportunity.
occulto (1), *tr.*, hide.
occupo (1), *tr.*, seize, occupy.

oculus, -i, *m.*, eye.
odi, odisse, *defect. tr.*, hate.
odium, -i, *n.*, hatred.
offensio, -onis, *f.*, accident, misfortune, failure.
omitto, -misi, -missum (3), *tr.*, pass over, disregard.
omnis, -e, all, every.
onus, -eris, *n.*, burden, load.
opera, -ae, *f.*, effort, service, help.
opimus, -a, -um, rich.
opinio, -onis, *f.*, opinion, belief.
opinor (1), *tr. and intr.*, think.
oportet, -uit (2), *impers.*, it is necessary, right, proper.
oppidum, -i, *n.*, town.
opportunitas, -atis, *f.*, favourable opportunity.
opprimo, -pressi, -pressum (3), *tr.*, crush, overwhelm, take by surprise.
oppugno (1), *tr.*, assault.
[ops] opis, *f.*, aid, help; *plur.*, resources, might, power.
optime, *adv.*, in the best way, best.
optimus, -a, -um, *superl. adj.*, best.
opto (1), *tr.*, wish for, desire.
ora, -ae, *f.*, border, coast, country.
oratio, -onis, *f.*, speech, language, eloquence.
orbis, -is, *m.*, circle; **orbis terrarum,** the world.
ordo, -inis, *m.*, order, rank, class.
ornamentum, -i, *n.*, equipment, decoration, distinction.
ornate, *adv.*, elegantly.
ornatus, -a, -um, distinguished, illustrious.
orno (1), *tr.*, fit out, equip, decorate, honour.

ostendo, -di, -tum (3), *tr.*, show, display.
ostium, -i, *n.*, door, mouth, entrance.

pacatus, -a, -um, pacified, peaceful.
par, paris, equal.
paratus, -a, -um, prepared, equipped.
parens, -ntis, *c.*, parent.
pareo, -ui (2), *intr. with dat.*, obey.
paro (1), *tr.*, prepare.
pars, partis, *f.*, part, party, side; *aliqua ex parte*, to some extent.
partim, *adv.*, partly.
parum, *adv.*, too little, not enough.
parvolus, -a, -um, tiny, insignificant.
parvus, -a, -um, small, little.
pastio, -onis, *f.*, pasture.
patefacio, -feci, -factum (3), *tr.*, open.
pateo, -ui (2), *intr.*, am open, lie open.
pater, patris, *m.*, father; *plur.*, ancestors.
patior, passus sum (3), *tr.*, suffer, allow.
patrius, -a, -um, of a father, hereditary, ancestral.
pauci, -ae, -a, few.
paulo, *adv.*, a little.
pax, pacis, *f.*, peace.
pecu, *plur.*, **pecua,** *n.*, cattle.
pecunia, -ae, *f.*, money.
pello, pepuli, pulsum (3), *tr.*, drive back, rout.
penitus, *adv.*, deeply.
pensito (1), *tr.*, pay.
per, *prep. with acc.*, through, by means of.

peradulescens, -ntis, very young.
perbrevis, -e, very short.
perditus, -a, -um, hopeless, desperate.
perdo, -didi, -ditum (3), *tr.*, destroy.
perfectus, -a, -um, finished, complete, perfect.
perfero, -ferre, -tuli, -latum, *tr.*, bring.
perficio, -feci, -fectum (3), *tr.*, finish.
perfugium, -i, *n.*, refuge.
periculosus, -a, -um, dangerous.
periculum, -i, *n.*, danger.
periniquus, -a, -um, very unfair.
peritus, -a, -um, *with gen.*, experienced, skilled in.
permagnus, -a, -um, very great.
permaneo, -mansi, -mansum (2), *intr.*, remain.
permitto, -misi, -missum (3), *tr.*, allow, let, permit, entrust.
permultum, *adv.*, very much.
permultus, -a, -um, very much, very many.
perpetuus, -a, -um, lasting.
persequor, -secutus sum (3), *tr.*, pursue, avenge, achieve, perform.
perseverantia, -ae, *f.*, perseverance.
perspicio, -spexi, -spectum (3), *tr.*, see clearly.
pertimesco, -timui (3), *tr.*, fear greatly.
pertineo, -tinui, -tentum (2), *intr.*, belong, concern, refer to.
pervado, -vasi, -vasum (3), *intr.*, spread.
pervenio, -veni, -ventum (4), *intr.*, come to, reach.

plebs, plebis *or* plebi, *f.*, the Plebeians.

plenus, -a, -um, full.

plurimum, *superl. adv.*, very much, very greatly.

plurimus, -a, -um, most, very many.

plus, pluris, *noun and comp. adv.*, more; *plur. adj.*, plures, -a, more.

poena, -ae, *f.*, punishment.

poeta, -ae, *m.*, poet.

polliceor (2), *tr. and intr.*, promise.

pono, posui, positum (3), *tr.*, put, place.

populus, -i, *m.*, people.

portus, -us, *m.*, harbour.

positus, -a, -um, placed, situated.

possum, posse, potui, *intr.*, am able.

post, *prep. with acc.*, after.

postea, *adv.*, afterwards.

posteaquam, *conj.*, after.

postremo, *superl. adv.*, finally, last of all.

postulo (1), *tr.*, demand.

potens, -ntis, powerful.

potestas, -atis, *f.*, power, authority.

potissimum, *superl. adv.*, especially.

praeceptum, -i, *n.*, rule, command.

praecipuus, -a, -um, special, extraordinary.

praeclarus, -a, -um, remarkable, distinguished.

praeda, -ae, *f.*, booty.

praedico (1), *tr.*, proclaim.

praeditus, -a, -um, endowed with, provided with.

praedo, -onis, *m.*, pirate.

praefero, -ferre, -tuli, -latum, *tr.*, put before, prefer.

praeficio, -feci, -fectum (3), *tr.*, set over, make commander of.

praepono, -posui, -positum (3), *tr.*, place in command of.

praescribo, -scripsi, -scriptum (3), *tr.*, order, command, appoint.

praesens, -ntis, present.

praesertim, *adv.*, principally, especially.

praesideo, -sedi (2), *intr. with dat.*, guard.

praesidium, -i, *n.*, guard, garrison.

praesto, -stiti, -stitum (1), *tr.*, be responsible for, guarantee.

praesum, praeesse, praefui, *intr. with dat.*, am in command of.

praeter, *prep with acc.*, beyond, contrary to, in addition to.

praeterea, *adv.*, besides.

praetereo, -ire, -ii, -itum, *tr.*, pass by.

praeteritus, -a, -um, gone by, past.

praetor, -oris, *m.*, praetor.

praetorius, -a, -um, of a praetor.

premo, pressi, pressum (3), *tr.*, press, press down, press hard.

primum, *adv.*, first.

primus, -a, -um, first; in primis, particularly.

princeps, -ipis, *m.*, chief man, leader.

principium, -i, *n.*, beginning.

privatus, -a, -um, private.

privatus, -i, *m.*, private citizen.

pro, *prep. with abl.*, for, on behalf of, in place of, in accordance with, by virtue of.

pro, *interj.*, oh!

procul, *adv.*, far off.

prodo, -didi, -ditum (3), *tr.*, publish, relate, record.

proelium, -i, *n.*, battle.

profecto, *adv.*, assuredly.

proficiscor, -fectus sum (3), *intr.*, start, set out.

profiteor, -fessus sum (2), *tr.*, declare publicly.

profugio, -fugi (3), *intr.*, flee, escape.

progressio, -onis, *f.*, advance.

progressus, -us, *m.*, advance.

prohibeo (2), *tr.*, prevent; defend, protect.

promulgo (1), *tr.*, promulgate, publish, propose a measure.

prope, *adv.*, nearly; *prep. with acc.*, near.

propono, -posui, -positum (3), *tr.*, put before, propose.

proprius, -a, -um, peculiar to, characteristic of.

propter, *adv.*, near, close at hand; *prep. with acc.*, near, on account of.

propterea, *adv.*, for this reason.

propterea quod, *conj.*, because.

propugnaculum, -i, *n.*, bulwark, outwork, defence.

prosterno, -stravi, -stratum (3), *tr.*, overthrow, destroy.

provideo, -vidi, -visum (2), *tr.*, foresee, see to, attend to.

provincia, -ae, *f.*, province.

provoco (1), *tr.*, call out, challenge.

proximus, -a, -um, nearest, last, next.

prudentia, -ae, *f.*, discretion, prudence, wisdom.

publicanus, -i, *m.*, tax-farmer.

publicus, -a, -um, public.

pudet, puduit *or* **puditum est** (2),

impers., it makes ashamed; *with acc.* of the person feeling the shame and the *gen.* of the cause.

pudor, -oris, *m.*, conscience, sense of honour.

pueritia, -ae, *f.*, boyhood.

pugna, -ae, *f.*, battle.

pugno (1), *intr.*, fight.

pulcher, -chra, -chrum, beautiful, fine, glorious.

puto (1), *tr.*, think.

quaero, quaesivi, quaesitum (3), *tr.*, seek, acquire, ask for.

quaestor, -oris, *m.*, quaestor.

quaestus, -us, *m.*, gain, profit.

qualis, -e, of what sort?; such as.

quam, *adv.*, how, than, as.

quamquam, *conj.*, although.

quantum, *noun or adv.*, how much?; as much as.

quantus, -a, -um, how great?; **tantus ... quantus,** as great as.

quasi, *conj.*, as if.

quattuor, *indecl. adj.*, four.

-que, *conj.*, and.

querimonia, -ae, *f.*, complaint.

queror, questus sum (3), *tr. and intr.*, complain, lament.

qui, quae, quod, *rel. pron.*, who, which.

qui, quae, quod, *interrog. adj.*, which?, what?

quicumque, quaecumque, quodcumque, whoever, whatever.

quidam, quaedam, quoddam, a certain.

quidem, *adv.*, indeed; **ne ... quidem,** not ... even.

quies, -etis, f., rest, repose.

quin, *conj.*, that not, but that, but, without *and verbal noun.*

quis, quid, *indef. pron.,* anyone, anything.

quis, quid, *interrog. pron.,* who?, what?; **quid,** *adv.,* why?

quisnam, quidnam, who?, what?

quisquam, quicquam, anyone, anything.

quisque, quaeque, quodque, each.

quisquis, quicquid, whoever, whatever.

quo, *adv. and conj.,* whither, why, because, that.

quocumque, *adv.,* to whatever place.

quod, *conj.,* because, that; **quod si,** but if.

quominus, *conj.,* that not.

quondam, *adv.,* formerly.

quoniam, *conj.,* since, because.

quoque, *conj.,* also.

quot, *indecl. adj.,* how many?; **tot . . . quot,** as many as.

quotannis, *adv.,* yearly.

rapio, rapui, raptum (3), *tr.,* seize and carry away, hurry away.

ratio, -onis, *f.,* account, transaction, business, affair, concern, care, manner, plan, calculation, judgement, reason.

recipio, -cepi, -ceptum (3), *tr.,* take back; *with reflex. pron.,* go back, retire.

reclamo (1), *intr.,* cry out, protest.

recordor (1), *tr. and intr.,* recollect.

recreo (1), *tr.,* restore.

recte, *adv.,* rightly.

recupero (1), *tr.,* regain, recover.

redimo, -emi, -emptum (3), *tr.,* buy back, ransom.

reditus, -us, *m.,* return.

redundo (1), *intr.,* overflow.

refercio, -si, -tum (4), *tr.,* fill, pack full.

refero, referre, rettuli, relatum, *tr.,* bring before, make a proposal, propose.

refert, referre, retulit, *impers. intr.,* it matters, it concerns.

refuto (1), *tr.,* refute, disprove.

regalis, -e, of a king, royal.

regio, -onis, *f.,* district, region.

regius, -a, -um, of a king, against a king.

regno (1), *intr.,* am king, reign.

regnum, -i, *n.,* kingdom.

rego, rexi, rectum (3), *tr.,* guide, rule.

religiosus, -a, -um, sacred, holy.

relinquo, -liqui, -lictum (3), *tr.,* leave, pass over, abandon.

reliquus, -a, -um, remaining, left.

remex, -igis, *m.,* rower.

remoror (1), *tr.,* delay.

renovo (1), *tr.,* renew, start again.

renuntio (1), *tr.,* report, announce.

repello, reppuli, repulsum (3), *tr.,* drive back, repel.

repente, *adv.,* suddenly.

reporto (1), *tr.,* carry back, win, gain.

reprimo, -pressi, -pressum (3), *tr.,* check, keep back.

repugno (1), *tr.,* oppose, resist.

requiro, -quisivi, -quisitum (3), *tr.,* seek for, need, lack, require.

res, rei, *f.,* thing, matter, affair, property, interest, cause; **res publica,** the state; **qua re,** wherefore.

respondeo, -di, -sum (2), *tr. and intr.,* answer.

resto, -stiti (1), *intr.*, am left, remain.

retardo (1), *tr.*, hinder, delay.

retineo, -tinui, -tentum (2), *tr.*, retain.

revoco (1), *tr.*, recall.

rex, -gis, *m.*, king.

robur, -oris, *n.*, strength.

rogatu, *m.*, request (*abl. sing. only*).

rogo (1), *tr.*, ask.

rumor, -oris, *m.*, report.

ruo, rui, rutum (3), *intr.*, collapse, fall in ruins.

saepe, *adv.*, often; **saepius,** *comp. adv.*, more often, very often.

saltus, -us, *m.*, woodland-pasture.

salus, -utis, *f.*, safety.

salvus, -a, -um, safe.

sanctus, -a, -um, sacred, inviolable.

sanguis, -inis, *m.*, blood.

sapiens, -ntis, wise.

sapientia, -ae, *f.*, wisdom.

satis, *adv. or noun,* enough, enough of.

scelus, -eris, *n.*, crime.

sciens, -ntis, skilled, expert.

scientia, -ae, *f.*, knowledge.

scio (4), *tr. and intr.*, know.

scribo, -psi, -ptum (3), *tr.*, write.

scriptura, -ae, *f.*, tax paid for use of public pasture land.

se *or* **sese, sui,** *third pers. reflex. pron.*, self.

secundus, -a, -um, following, second, favourable, successful.

securis, -is, *f.*, axe.

sed, *conj.*, but.

seiungo, -nxi, -nctum (3), *tr.*, separate.

semper, *adv.*, always.

senatorius, -a, -um, of a senator, senatorial.

senatus, -us, *m.*, senate.

sententia, -ae, *f.*, opinion.

sentio, sensi, sensum (4), *tr.*, feel, perceive, think.

sepelio, sepelivi, sepultum (4), *tr.*, bury.

sermo, -onis, *m.*, talk, conversation, report, rumour.

servilis, -e, of a slave, servile.

servio (4), *intr. with dat.*, serve.

servitus, -utis, *f.*, slavery.

severus, -a, -um, stern, strict, severe.

si, *conj.*, if.

sic, *adv.*, so, thus.

sicut *or* **sicuti,** *adv.*, just as.

significatio, -onis, *f.*, indication, signal.

signum, -i, *n.*, statue, standard; **signa conferre,** fight in battle.

similiter, *adv.*, in like manner.

simulatio, -onis, *f.*, pretence.

simulo (1), *tr.*, pretend.

simultas, -atis, *f.*, rivalry, jealousy, enmity.

sin, *conj.*, but if.

sine, *prep. with abl.*, without.

singularis, -e, unique, remarkable, outstanding.

singuli, -ae, -a, one each, single.

sino, sivi, situm (3), *tr.*, allow.

sinus, -us, *m.*, bay.

socius, -i, *m.*, ally.

soleo, solitus sum (2), *intr.*, am accustomed.

solum, *adv.*, only.

solus, -a, -um, alone, only.

solutio, -onis, *f.*, payment.

solvo, solvi, solutum (3), *tr.*, free, release.

speculato₁, -oris, *m*., spy.

spero (1), *tr*., hope, expect.

spes, -ei, *f*., hope.

spiritus, -us, *m*., breath; *plur*., haughtiness, pride, arrogance.

splendor, -oris, *m*., splendour, magnificence.

spolio (1), *tr*., rob.

spolium, -i, *n*., spoil, booty.

statim, *adv*., immediately.

statuo, statui, statutum (3), *tr*., establish, decide, resolve, appoint.

stipendium, -i, *n*., pay, military service, campaign.

studiose, *adv*., eagerly.

studium, -i, *n*., zeal, eagerness, goodwill.

subsidium, -i, *n*., support, help.

succedo, -cessi, -cessum (3), *intr*. *with dat*., succeed to.

suffragium, -i, *n*., vote.

sum, esse, fui, am.

summus, -a, -um, highest, greatest, most distinguished.

sumo, sumpsi, sumptum (3), *tr*., take.

sumptus, -us, *m*., expense, cost.

superbe, *adv*., arrogantly, insolently.

superior, -us, higher, former.

supero (1), *tr*., conquer.

supplex, -icis, suppliant.

supplicium, -i, *n*., punishment, pain, suffering.

suscipio, -cepi, -ceptum (3), *tr*., incur, undertake, suffer.

suus, -a, -um, one's own, his own etc.

tabula, -ae, *f*., picture.

tacitus, -a, -um, silent.

taeter, -tra, -trum, foul, horrible, shameful, abominable.

talis, -e, such.

tam, *adv*., so, so much.

tamen, *conj*., nevertheless, however.

tametsi, *conj*., although.

tandem, *adv*., at length, pray.

tantum, *adv*., so much.

tantus, -a, -um, so great, so much.

tardo (1), *tr*., delay.

tectum, -i, *n*., roof, house.

tego, -xi, -ctum (3), *tr*., cover, protect, defend.

temere, *adv*., at random, rashly.

temperantia, -ae, *f*., moderation, self-control.

tempestas, -atis, *f*., storm.

tempestivus, -a, -um, seasonable, suitable.

templum, -i, *n*., temple.

tempto (1), *tr*., attack.

tempus, -oris, *n*., time; *plur*., the times, circumstances, emergency.

teneo (2), *tr*., hold, control.

tenuis, -e, thin, weak, poor.

ter, *adv*., three times.

terra, -ae, *f*., land.

terror, -oris, *m*., terror, panic.

tertius, -a, -um, third.

testis, -is, *c*., witness.

testor (1), *tr*., call to witness.

timeo (2), *tr. and intr*., fear.

timide, *adv*., timidly.

timor, -oris, *m*., fear.

tollo, sustuli, sublatum (3), *tr*., take away, remove.

tot, *indecl. adj*., so many.

totus, -a, -um, whole.

tracto (1), *tr*., treat, handle.

trado, -didi, -ditum (3), *tr*., hand down, pass on.

traho, traxi, tractum (3), *tr.*, drag, draw.

transmarinus, -a, -um, beyond the sea.

transmitto, -misi, -missum (3), *tr. and intr.*, send across, transfer; cross.

tres, tria, three.

tribunus (plebi), -i, *m.*, tribune of the plebs; **tribunus (militum),** military tribune.

tribuo, -ui, -utum (3), *tr.*, assign, grant, give.

triumpho (1), *intr.*, triumph.

triumphus, -i, *m.*, triumph.

trucido (1), *tr.*, butcher.

tu, tui, you.

tueor (2), *tr.*, watch over, guard, protect.

tum, *adv.*, then.

turpis, -e, disgraceful, dishonourable.

turpitudo, -inis, *f.*, disgrace.

tutus, -a, -um, safe.

ubertas, -atis, *f.*, richness, fertility.

ubique, *adv.*, everywhere.

ullus, -a, -um, any.

ultimus, -a, -um, furthest.

umquam, *adv.*, ever.

una, *adv.*, together.

unde, *adv.*, whence, from which.

undequinquagesimus, -a, -um, forty-ninth.

undique, *adv.*, on all sides.

universus, -a, -um, whole, as a whole, general.

unus, -a, -um, one, only.

urbs, -is, *f.*, city.

usquam, *adv.*, anywhere.

usque, *adv.*, all the way to *or* from, continually, always.

usus, -us, *m.*, use, practice, exercise, experience, custom.

ut, *conj.*, *and adv.*, as, how, when, in order that, so that, that.

uterque, utraque, utrumque, each (of two).

utilitas, -atis, *f.*, usefulness, advantage, expediency.

utinam, *adv.*, would that!

utor, usus sum (3), *intr. with abl.*, use, experience, have the use of, enjoy.

utrum, *interrog. adv.*, whether.

vacuus, -a, -um, empty, free from.

valeo (2), *intr.*, am strong, powerful.

varietas, -atis, *f.*, variety.

varius, -a, -um, various, diverse.

vectigal, -alis, *n.*, tax, tribute.

vectigalis, tributary; **vectigales, -ium,** *m. plur.*, tributaries.

vehemens, -ntis, strong, powerful.

vehementer, *adv.*, vigorously.

vel, *adv. and conj.*, even, or.

veneo, -ire, -ii, -itum, *intr.*, am for sale, am sold.

venia, -ae, *f.*, pardon.

venio, veni, ventum (4), *intr.* come.

ventus, -i, *m.*, wind.

ver, veris, *n.*, spring.

verber, -eris, *n.*, stripe, lash, blow.

verbum, -i, *n.*, word.

vere, *adv.*, truly.

veritas, -atis, *f.*, truth.

vero, *adv.*, in truth, but.

versor (1), *intr.*, am situated, am engaged in, am occupied with.

verum, *adv.*, truly.

verus, -a, -um, true.

vester, -tra, -trum, your.

vestigium, -i, *n.*, footstep.

vetus, -eris, old.

via, -ae, *f.*, way, road.

vicesimus, -a, -um, twentieth.

victor, -oris, victorious, conqueror.

victoria, -ae, *f.*, victory.

videlicet, *adv.*, clearly, obviously, of course.

video, vidi, visum (2), *tr.*, see; *pass.*, seem, seem right.

vigilo (1), *intr.*, am awake, am watchful.

vilitas, -atis, *f.*, cheapness.

vinco, vici, victum (3), *tr.*, conquer.

vinculum, -i, *n.*, chain, fetter.

violo (1), *tr.*, do violence to, injure, outrage.

vir, viri, *m.*, man.

virtus, -utis, *f.*, strength, vigour, goodness, merit, bravery, valour.

vis, *acc.*, vim, *abl.*, vi, *f.*, force, quantity, number; vires, -ium, *plur.*, strength.

viso, -si, -sum (3), *tr.*, look at, go to see, visit.

vita, -ae, *f.*, life.

vitium, -i, *n.*, fault.

vivo, vixi, victum (3), *intr.*, live.

vix, *adv.*, hardly, scarcely.

voco (1), *tr.*, call, place (*in a certain condition or position*).

volo, velle, volui, *tr. and intr.*, wish, wish for, am willing.

voluntas, -atis, *f.*, wish, will, good will.

voluptas, -atis, *f.*, pleasure.

vosmet, *emphatic plur. of* tu.

vox, vocis, *f.*, voice.

vulgo, *adv.*, generally, universally, commonly.

vulnus, -eris, *n.*, wound.

INDEXES

I. PROPER NAMES

2. Notes on Accidence and Syntax

ablative
  form of present participle, 64
  of agent with gerundive, 41, 67
  of attendant circumstances, 62
  of description, 61
  instrumental, 57, 61, 65, 66, 71, 77
  of measure of difference, 77
  of place without preposition, 48
  of respect, 71
  of separation, 34, 57
accusative
  internal, 86

antecedent, attracted into relative clause, 68
antithesis, xvii, 35, 48
attraction of tense, 44

chiasmus, xvii, 45, 63
commutatio, xvii, 65, 86
cum, temporal with past indicative, 54, 71, 78, 82

dative
  of agent, 52, 53, 63, 88
  predicative, 52

3. NOTES ON HISTORICAL AND POLITICAL BACKGROUND